Molly burst into flames, then exploded, and that was only a hint of the kind of heat that Constantine's mouth on hers generated.

It was only the start.

Her hands came up of their own accord, fluttering near his shoulders when she had never *fluttered* a day in her life. He was so big all around her when she was used to towering over most men. His mouth was so *hot*. And he angled his jaw as his tongue swept hers, making her shiver out as well as in.

His kiss was slick, wicked and insidious, and almost unbearably good.

He kissed the way he did everything. Lazy, reckless and, underneath it all, a dark edge of that same danger she really should have heeded.

She could taste him. Smell him. His tongue was a temptation, his sensual mouth a seduction, and she could hardly make sense of all the sensations that stormed in her.

Molly was lost.

Rich, Ruthless & Greek

Temptation and passion may just topple these ruthless billionaires...

Ruthless billionaire brothers Balthazar and Constantine Skalas have had a hard path to the top. And despite their hatred for one another, they've turned their small family enterprise into a billion-dollar business. Now they must unite to get the revenge they've been waiting so patiently to exact for the wrongs of their past!

Only two enigmatic women interrupt their mission. Because what these powerful tycoons never realized before is that passion can be *so* powerful—and distracting...

Read Balthazar's story in
The Secret That Can't Be Hidden

Read Constantine's story in
A Deal with the Greek Devil

Caitlin Crews

HER DEAL WITH THE
GREEK DEVIL

HARLEQUIN
PRESENTS

HARLEQUIN®
PRESENTS®

Recycling programs
for this product may
not exist in your area.

ISBN-13: 978-1-335-40409-1

Her Deal with the Greek Devil

Copyright © 2021 by Caitlin Crews

Harlequin Enterprises ULC
22 Adelaide St. West, 40th Floor
Toronto, Ontario M5H 4E3, Canada
www.Harlequin.com

Printed in U.S.A.

USA TODAY bestselling and RITA® Award–nominated author **Caitlin Crews** loves writing romance. She teaches her favorite romance novels in creative-writing classes at places like UCLA Extension's prestigious Writers' Program, where she finally gets to utilize the MA and PhD in English literature she received from the University of York in England. She currently lives in the Pacific Northwest with her very own hero and too many pets. Visit her at caitlincrews.com.

Books by Caitlin Crews

Harlequin Presents

Chosen for His Desert Throne

Once Upon a Temptation

Claimed in the Italian's Castle

Passion in Paradise

The Italian's Pregnant Cinderella

Royal Christmas Weddings

Christmas in the King's Bed
His Scandalous Christmas Princess

Rich, Ruthless & Greek

The Secret That Can't Be Hidden

Visit the Author Profile page
at Harlequin.com for more titles.

CHAPTER ONE

CONSTANTINE SKALAS HAD waited a long, long time for this day. What had started as a young man's rash promise had become a plot. Then a plan. Today that plan had finally borne its intended fruit.

He intended to savor it.

And as a man who had dedicated a large portion of his decidedly debaucherous adult life to relishing all the many pleasures life had in store, he knew precisely how best to go about it.

There were any number of places he could have met the object of all his many plans. He was a Skalas, one of two owners of the sprawling, multinational Skalas & Sons. His father had once been the richest man alive, but Constantine and his brother, Balthazar, had doubled his wealth within the first year of their ownership. He had properties literally everywhere, homes and rentals and hotels, and could have chosen any one of them for today's long-awaited meeting.

Naturally, he'd chosen the one calculated to stick the knife in, and he hoped, give it a little twist for good measure. It was an estate in the quiet part of Skiathos, an island off the coast of Thessaly, Greece. Skiathos, where far too many bright young things flocked for the energetic nightlife in Skiathos Town, though Constantine had not availed himself of the local amenities, or talent, in longer than he cared to recall. And Skiathos was also where, once upon a time, he had been force-fed his father's new and unacceptable second wife and worse, had been required to contend with an awkward stepsister he had never warmed to in the slightest.

Though that was perhaps understating the case.

He had despised his stepmother. He had felt only slightly less opposed to his stepsister, who might not have been at fault for her mother's ambitious marriage—but she hadn't done anything to oppose it, either. Those feelings had not dimmed over time. His father might have thought better of his second marriage and summarily ended it, as he had been wont to do with his customary brutality, but Constantine could hold a grudge until the end of time.

And did. Happily.

He settled back in the chair behind the desk where the late and wholly unlamented Demetrius Skalas, his father, had once conducted his business when he'd called this house his primary home. It had been but a few years of madness before Demetrius had rid himself of the appalling British housekeeper, Isabel, and her hopeless daughter that he'd acquired for reasons unclear. As far as Constantine could tell, Demetrius had only married Isabel in the first place to really hammer home the fact he was moving on from his elegant and fragile first wife. The wife he'd crushed, then discarded, then mocked as she'd cycled deep into despair.

The wife who happened to be Constantine's mother, that was.

But Constantine was not going to think about his mother today, or he would lose his cool. And his quarry did not deserve his temper. She did not deserve to see anything but his vengeance.

He studied his father's desk as he sat there. Like all the things Demetrius had used as props to bolster his inflated sense of himself, the desk was a monstrosity. Constantine had entirely too many memories of being forced to stand on the other side of this very desk during those years, his eyes on his father if he valued his hide, while he gave a twenty-year-old's surly accounting of what he'd done with his monthly allowance. A tedious undertaking when he already knew it would lead to more of his father's brand of consequences. And all the while the wall of windows down one side—all of which opened up as doors to the terrace no one was permitted to use without Demetrius's never-proffered permission—let in the pine-covered cliffs. Unusual for Greek islands, as the tourists liked to caterwaul, but pine trees they were and they rose above the private cove the house sat over like the king Demetrius had imagined he was. And more, the great Aegean beyond beckoned, all while Constantine had been required to stand still and pretend penitence.

It had been torture, in other words.

A torture he intended to visit upon dear stepsister, Molly, who his staff down at the gate to the estate had informed him had just arrived.

The waiting was exquisite.

After all these years, after all his plotting, after creating the perfect disguise for his true intentions and living it in full view of the world, it was time.

If he was capable of such things, he might have considered himself positively gleeful.

Constantine leaned back in the huge leather chair, itself a monument to a certain kind of overt masculinity. His father's kind, all bluster and bark, but unlike some of his toxic ilk, with a deadly bite beneath.

His father had died a few years back, and unlike Constantine's older brother, Balthazar, who had always splayed himself wide open with an unnecessary sense of responsibility, Constantine did not miss him. Perish the thought. The world was a far better place without Demetrius Skalas. His sons, in particular, were incalculably better off without him.

Not to mention, the old man's absence meant Constantine had finally been able to put the plan closest to his blackened heart into action.

He waited, smiling to himself when he heard the click of very high heels along the hallway floors that led to this study. He had not known which version of his stepsister to expect. But the heels were like a premonition, and then, in the next moment, she appeared.

She stopped in the doorway and regarded him.

Constantine gazed right back, aware of a certain electrical charge that seemed to fill the space between them.

No longer awkward or embarrassing, or anything like gawky, little Molly Payne, the housekeeper's daughter had transformed herself. She stood before him, framed by the doorway, and stared at him as if she stood atop some kind of catwalk and he was at her feet. It was adorable, truly. And he had seen her blond hair in a number of different styles, but today she had gone for big and lustrous curls, like a cat puffing itself up to make itself seem bigger in the face of a predator.

Poor little kitty, he thought to himself, darkly. *Your tricks and claws will not help you here.*

Her eyes were a stunning, arctic blue, and today

she'd expertly applied the kind of cosmetics that took hours to achieve a barely there look, so that she looked effortlessly sultry, the cold color of those eyes honed to a laser point. Her pout was enough to raze cities to the ground, and that wasn't getting to her magnificent figure that had been splashed across every magazine cover in existence, then back again.

For awkward little Molly Payne had not had the good manners to fade off into obscurity when her mother's reprehensible marriage to Constantine's father had ended. He had imagined she would lead a perfectly unobjectionable porridge sort of life, perhaps away in one of those sad, lesser British cities, where everything was forever gray and depressed. Like she had been.

But no such luck. For instead, his stepsister had gone ahead and had the temerity to become universally, stratospherically famous.

"If it isn't the eponymous *Magda*," Constantine drawled, eventually, using her laughable professional name.

"Hello, Constantine," she replied.

Like all beautiful women whose looks were widely held to be objective fact, not subject to individual opinion, every inch of her was weaponized. Including that voice. It struck him like his favorite spirit, METAXA, smooth and complex before rolling on into a deeper, hotter intensity.

He had expected to feel the attraction that hammered him then, but it was far worse now that she was in this room than it usually was when he was confronted with her picture. Everywhere.

"I thought you would enjoy this trip down memory lane with me," he said, lounging back in the chair. His father had been a rigid man, his only excesses brutal. Constantine, by contrast, had created for himself the most dissipated, dissolute alter ego possible. It had started when he was young. He had learned, as his brother never had, that there was no point in attempting to live up to a madman's expectations. For every time a certain level was achieved, their father made up seven more. No one could possibly scale those heights.

Constantine had stopped trying. Then and now, he took great pleasure in polluting his father's legacy with his own brand of what he liked to call his libertine approach to rakishness.

The tabloids used other words. He delighted in all of them.

"Is that what this is?" Molly asked. For he refused to think of her as *Magda*. "Memory lane? Funny, that. This particular road to hell always seemed remarkably unpaved to me."

"How droll. You've become so spiky over the years."

She did not shift from where she stood, shown to perfection in the doorway to the study. And

Constantine had taken on a deep, personal study of the rise of Magda, a modern supermodel in a time when supermodels were widely held to be a thing of the past. He knew she was fully aware that the sun streamed in from without, lighting her beautifully, and dancing all over the exquisitely skintight gown she wore in a deliberately overbright shade of gold. The sunlight made her glow like an angelic host. He knew that she was well aware of the position in which she stood, designed to call attention to the impeccable lines of her body that left fashion designers beside themselves as they draped their latest creations all over her frame. Here, in this study, she simply looked magnificent. And untouchable.

Too bad for her that he had other ideas.

"Everyone grows up, Constantine," she replied. She considered. "Or, I should say, almost everyone."

"Was that a dig?" He made a tsking sound. "That is no way to convince me to be merciful, Molly. You must know that."

"I would prefer it if you called me Magda."

He grinned, enjoying himself immensely. "I am certain that you would. But I think I will stick with Molly all the same. Just to remind ourselves who and what we are."

Fascinated, he watched as a storm moved

through that cool blue gaze of hers before she shuttered her gaze.

And then he waited, letting the silence spill out between them. Until, to his very great pleasure, she stopped holding that commanding position in the doorway and took a step farther into the room.

Betraying herself, he thought.

"I know you know why I'm here," she said, sounding far more brisk, then. "I suppose we might as well get down to business."

"Refresh my memory," he invited her.

"I see that we're going to play games. Lovely."

He remembered the sixteen-year-old who had foolishly confided in him and saw no trace of her on this woman's face. But that was just as well. Constantine did not traffic in guilt or shame, so he would never use those words to describe how he felt when he thought of that time. And yet sometimes it haunted him, all the same.

"Is that really necessary?" she asked.

"You will know what is necessary and what is unnecessary," he assured her. "Because I will tell you." He inclined his head, then waved a lazy hand. "For now, by all means, tell me your sad tale of woe, Molly."

"I do not wish to bore you." Her cool eyes glittered, like shards of ice, and he suspected she was thinking of a great many things she would like to

do to him, none of them boring. All of them vio-
lent. "I know you remember my mother."

"As it happens, I have known a great number of
grasping, petulant, jumped-up whores in my life,"
Constantine drawled, each word deliberate. Each
word its own sharp blade. "And yet, you are correct, your mother managed to distinguish herself."

A faint splash of color stained Molly's cheeks.
Her eyes blazed with fury. And he had the sudden,
near uncontrollable urge to rise from his chair,
throw himself across the room, and get his hands
and his mouth into all of that fire.

But too soon, she reined herself in, iced over,
and regarded him coolly once again.

Interesting, he thought. He would have to make
a note of how she protected herself with that aloof-
ness. And set it ablaze.

"I am not here to debate my mother's faults with
you, or anyone," she said crisply.

"And yet I feel certain that should I wish to discuss your mother's many faults and terrible decisions, I will. Entirely as I please. With or without
your permission. Molly."

She took a long, visible breath, but did not object. Because she was not a stupid woman, Constantine knew. And she was not in the dark as to
why she was here, any more than he was.

"My mother has always fancied herself a
businesswoman of sorts," Molly said, her voice

ever so slightly strained. She moved further into the study that he knew she hadn't seen since she was still a teenager. It was unchanged. He watched with interest as she took that in, her gaze moving with arctic precision from the ponderous choice of art on the walls to the crystal decanter on the sideboard, which was the last in a long line of similar decanters his father had shattered against the wall. Such pleasant memories. "This is not a business in the sense of Skalas & Sons, of course. What is? But whenever she found herself with some money—"

"Such as her divorce settlement," Constantine interjected silkily. "Three million euros to silently go away when she should have done so on her own, had she the faintest shred of shame."

Molly ignored that. He hoped it was hard. "She did some investing, here and there. And she began to imagine herself something of a hotel mogul."

"Surely that would be better termed a delusion and used to secure medical attention." Constantine laughed when Molly's frigid gaze swept to him. "I have many hotels. In my personal portfolio, not underneath the Skalas & Sons umbrella. I hardly think a few poorly chosen boutique options scattered about the globe make a mogul. But to each her own."

"Funny you should mention those few boutique hotels," Molly said softly, her gaze on him.

"Because, wouldn't you know it, she's completely overextended herself and faces total financial ruin, because someone leveraged them right out from under her."

"What a sad story this is," Constantine murmured. "How lucky she must be that she has an internationally famous daughter who she can lean upon for support in such troubled times. Troubled times she brought upon herself, but I digress."

"I hate to continually tell you things you already know," Molly said, her voice acidic. She picked up a photograph from one of the incidental tables. A seemingly happy family shot until one looked closer and saw the look of worry on young Balthazar's face, the mutiny on Constantine's, and their father's grim expression that promised retribution.

If he recalled correctly, that time, Demetrius had beaten them both.

Ah, the manifold joys of family, Constantine thought dryly.

"But I know so little," he said. "Ask anyone."

Molly turned back to him then, and her gaze was a little too clever for his liking. Only because clever women boded ill, always. It was his own personal curse that he preferred them.

Not that his usual choice of paramour would make that clear.

His typical selections bored him, but they were

beautiful. And the more vacant the woman on his arm, the more it was assumed that he, too, must also be shallow to his very core no matter how good he was at making money. He encouraged it.

Better that no one should ever see him coming.

"Since she left England to marry your father, my mother has always had one scheme or another," Molly told him. "Before these hotels, it was her own fashion line. Before the fashion line, she fell for at least three different scams."

He affected a vaguely sympathetic expression. "Con men abound."

"I used to think that she just had spectacularly bad luck," she agreed. She even smiled, though it was a cold curve of her famous lips. "Recent events have made it clear to me that no, she has one, very powerful enemy. And has always had this enemy."

Molly glared at him. Constantine grinned.

"That sounds ghastly," he said. "What do you suppose she might have done to gain such an enemy, if one exists?"

"Since you asked," Molly said, folding her arms before her, "she had the terrible misfortune of believing a horrible man when he claimed to be in love with her. Only in the end, lo and behold, it turned out he was not. But she only discovered that after a disastrous marriage that came complete with two unpleasant stepsons who made her life a living hell."

"Surely her choice of husband was the living hell she chose because it came alongside so much money," Constantine replied, his tone as smooth as it was dark. "These bargains are always so tawdry, are they not? But tell me, what sort of woman blames her stepchildren for her venal little choices?"

"Oh, you mistake me." Molly sounded as dark as he did, though three times as cold. And her gaze should have frozen him solid. "She doesn't blame anyone. *She* doesn't look back. But I do."

Constantine wanted to share his thoughts on the dreadful Isabel, Molly's mother, who should never have been permitted to set foot on Skalas property. Much less take up residence here. When all she should ever have been to Demetrius was a night's amusement. Possibly two. Who *married* the housekeeper after a weekend at a business acquaintance's old pile in the English countryside? Who then paraded about with a housekeeper on his arm?

Only Demetrius.

"Blame is such a funny thing, is it not?" he asked. "Oddly enough, I, too, have those I blame for the misfortunes that have befallen both me and my family. For my part, I find that what goes well with blame is power. For one is whining. The other is winning. And, Molly, you should know by now that I always, always win."

"I'm tired of playing this game," she replied, her gaze like ice. "You know that my mother is near enough to ruined and I'm on the verge of bankruptcy. You know it because you did it."

"I have had no interaction with you whatsoever since you were a depressed teenager," Constantine said mildly. "I suspect you are well aware that we've been at the same parties, from time to time, yet we somehow managed never to speak. How could I possibly be responsible for your inability to handle your finances?"

"She's my mother, Constantine." That was the first crack. The first hint of her emotions, and it was all he'd hoped for, a flash of deep, dark blue and that catch in her throat. "What am I supposed to do? Throw her out into the streets?"

He shrugged. "It sounds like that would be a good start if, as you say, she has had such…terrible luck."

Molly looked down for a moment and he thought he saw the faintest hint of a fine tremor move through her. Though it was gone so quickly, he couldn't be sure. And he didn't want to believe she was reacting quite in that way. Constantine only wanted her to feel the things he wanted her to feel. Not fall beneath the weight of them all. Where would be the fun in that?

For him, that was.

"I assume that this is what you wanted," she said after a moment, no sign of cracks or temper visible on her perfect face. "You left just enough clues. When I put the pieces together, it all made a kind of sick, strange sense. This whole playboy act of yours is just that. An act. You spend a lot of time and energy pretending a flashy car can turn your head and that you're as vapid as the interchangeable women you squire about. When the truth is, you're exactly as much of a shark as your brother, you just hide it. I'm sure you have your own, twisted reasons, as ever. I suppose it was silly of me to imagine that after making sure my teenage years were as hideous as possible, you would keep right on going."

"I think you'll find that teenage years, as a rule, are hideous for all." He smiled. "Even me. Though I am interested that both you and your mother seem to have no shortage of people to blame for your misfortunes. Anyone and everyone except yourselves, is that it?"

Again, a splash of color on her porcelain cheeks, but that was all that betrayed the emotions inside her. He was more fascinated than was wise, he knew that. But knowing it didn't change it any.

Molly regarded him as if he was the devil. It pleased him. "You set a trap and my mother walked right into it, over and over. Congratulations. Now why don't you tell me what it is you really want?"

So many things in life did not live up to expectations, Constantine knew. Most things deemed decadent, for example. The so-called charms of the yachting set who cluttered up the Mediterranean coastlines and bored him silly. Too many Michelin-starred restaurants, forever attempting to outwit their diners instead of simply feeding them. The notion that because a woman was beautiful to look at, she would be any good in bed.

But this. This was the exception that proved the truth.

For this was even better than he had imagined it—and he had imagined it in a thousand different variations, year after year.

"Why, I thought what I wanted was obvious," Constantine said, milking the moment for all it was worth.

Because he had waited all this time. Because his mother lay senseless in a long-term care facility, dead in all but name thanks to what had been done to her. Balthazar had handled the architect of their mother's downfall, the man who had seduced her then discarded her, then laughed when their father had done the same. Constantine was glad his brother had taken care of that egregious loose end. But for his part, he had never forgiven the woman who had truly imagined she could walk in and take their mother's place.

"Spell it out for me," Molly urged him. "I know you can't want my money, because you have far too much of your own. And anyway, all of my money is gone. Because someone had to take care of my mother's debts when you ruined her again and again—but I think you already know that. So what is it?"

"I told you when you called me, did I not? I do hate to repeat myself."

"In the very brief, *very* obnoxious phone call it took you three weeks to return, you told me that there was a possibility my mother could reclaim her properties and retain her good name, such as it was." Her blue eyes glinted. "Your words, obviously. I'm betting it will involve intense humiliation for all the world to see, that being your specialty. Just tell me the shape of it."

"Intensity and humiliation are all a question of degrees," Constantine mused. Philosophically. "And perspective, do you not think? It should be obvious what I want, Molly." He smiled. "It is the one thing I am truly known for."

And he had the great pleasure of watching her face go slack with shock. He saw, very clearly and distinctly, the difference between Molly and Magda, because she lost completely that harder shell he supposed she must have developed over the years. And in its place was the face of a girl he half remembered, wide blue eyes, a sulky mouth, and forever where she didn't belong.

"You can't mean…"

"But I do," he told her, his voice low and deliberate. Revenge served cold, and it made him hot, everywhere. "I want you, Molly. Beneath me. And above me. And in all other ways. Naked, begging, and most of all, completely mine to do with what I wish, for as long as I wish, until your mother's debt is paid. In full."

She actually gaped at him. His smile widened.

"Did I not tell you it was a simple thing?" he asked silkily. "You should know this above all else, Molly. I am nothing if not a man of my word."

CHAPTER TWO

MOLLY PAYNE WANTED to die.

A not unusual occurrence in this man's presence. Or in the presence of any member of the vile Skalas family, for that matter, though in the years since her mother's escape from their clutches she had tried to block out her reaction to actually *standing before* one of them.

She'd obviously grown soft over the past decade.

Because this was much, much worse than her memories.

As far as Molly was concerned, the Skalas family was a scourge upon the earth. A very rich, very powerful scourge. When she'd heard the news that cruel old Demetrius had died, though she did not make a habit of thinking ill of the dead under normal circumstances, Molly and her mother had gone out to a lovely meal in London to celebrate. That mean old bastard deserved a few toasts to speed him along to hell, where he belonged.

But Constantine was a special case.

He had always been the seemingly nice one. Where his father was cruel and his older brother, Balthazar, distant and disapproving, Constantine had been friendly. He had encouraged Molly, ungainly and terribly shy, to open up to him about what it was like to be the daughter of a woman like her mother. And she had told him, to her eternal shame. She had spent sixteen years filled with that desperate, helpless love on the one hand, yet cringing all the time at each and every obvious indication that Isabel Payne would do almost anything if she thought it would serve her ambition.

And the friendlier he was to her, the more Molly had told him things she should have kept to herself. Sacred, secret things she had no business sharing with anyone or anything but her own diary.

Things Constantine had gone right ahead and shared with the tabloids, and yet she had been so overawed by him that it had taken the better part of those terrible two years to fully accept that, yes, she was the source of all those gossipy stories about her mother's ghastly relationship with Demetrius Skalas. *Isabel's True Face Revealed*, and so on.

That was bad enough. Hideous, in fact. But such was his bitter genius that it had taken her many more years to realize that what he'd done to *her* was far more insidious than merely telling her secrets to a tabloid. Molly had come away from her mother's unhappy, if profitable, marriage to Demetrius Skalas convinced that she was a plodding, embarrassing bit of blancmange, destined for a quiet life of secretarial work, meals from a greasy local chippie with too much wine from the off-license, and the spiraling claws of despair. Had she not been discovered by a modeling agent on the Tube, of all the absurd stories she would have said were fake if it hadn't happened to her, she imagined that was precisely the life she would be living right this moment. As if those two short years in the Greek sun were a beautiful nightmare she'd had once, long ago while she lived out an un-remarkable existence somewhere far away from the concerns of the Skalas family.

She'd come to realize that he'd wanted that to be her fate.

Her curse was that she'd spent even longer than that trying to justify the things he'd said and the way he'd said them to relieve him of any respon-sibility. It was her fault, clearly. She should have made it more clear that the things she'd told him were private. She had misread him, or misheard him, or taken it all in wrong because—as everyone had reminded her all the time in those days—she was so *sensitive.*

But no. Over the last few years, as Molly had begun to understand that her mother, for all her faults, could not possibly be *quite this* unlucky, a different picture of Constantine Skalas had emerged.

Now she knew the truth. The nicest, most approachable Skalas brother was, in fact, the devil.

The tragedy was that, like Lucifer himself—not called Morning Star because he was deformed or horrible—Constantine was beautiful. Ridiculously, absurdly beautiful.

And he knew it.

Everything about him was dark and rich and seductive. Dark brown hair that glinted gold in the Greek sun and always looked as if fingers not his own had moments before raked through it. His eyes were heavy-lidded and suggestive, as impossibly dark and yet inviting as the bitter coffee he preferred. And he used his unfair cheekbones to their full effect, always. He had a generous, sensual mouth that was forever curving with a hint of wickedness. Or grinning widely without a care. Or more often still, laughing lazily at all the women who flailed about at his feet, all the lovers who trailed behind him weeping and wailing and clinging to his trouser cuff, and the whole of the great and glorious world that loved him all the more when he treated everything and everyone in it as his.

As one of the Skalas brothers and thus one of the wealthiest men alive, the truth was that much of the world really was.

And for a man who never seemed to do anything but lounge about, languid and bedroom-eyed, Constantine was obnoxiously fit. He was unnecessarily tall and rangy, with long, lean muscles that he was forever showing off. Glistening his way across exclusive seaside resorts, shedding his shirt to crash a game of footie in the park, leaping in and out of the odd plane yet living, propping up beautiful women on his black-tied arm, and always infusing all of his nearly overwhelming sexual energy with more than a hint of lurking danger.

That was just the grainy pictures in the magazines. Constantine in person was…worse. He had been shockingly attractive when they were younger, something Molly had tried to tell herself had been something she'd made up because she'd been such a young and foolish sixteen. But there had been nothing wrong with her eyes back then. He had been feral and gorgeous, always. And now, all of those relatively softer edges and blurred angles had disappeared entirely.

Leaving him relentlessly, ruthlessly, inarguably masculine. Every last inch honed to brutal, sensual effect.

And that was not the only tragedy.

Molly's deep and abiding shame was that even now, after all she knew about Constantine Skalas and all he'd done—and had yet to do to her, personally—she still had only to think about him and she felt everything inside her...melt.

She was pathetic.

Especially because, despite everything, she had not been adequately prepared for the reality of seeing him in his considerably mouthwatering flesh today. What was *wrong* with her? Maybe he'd been right all along when he'd suggested to the impressionable girl she'd been that she was simply wired wrong.

"Struck dumb in the face of my generosity?" he asked, sounding lazy and amused, as always. "I do not blame you. Being my mistress is a privilege, I grant you. Even under these vulgar circumstances, it would, naturally, constitute quite an elevation for you."

"Your mistress," Molly repeated.

Her mind couldn't take that on, much less the other insults packed into his words. She couldn't actually let herself visualize what *being his mistress* entailed because it was too much. It was an explosion of golden limbs and heat and his mouth...

Stop it, she ordered herself. *Dear God.*

And though it hurt, physically, she pulled herself together. Or tried. "Right. You want a shag. If I was paid for every man who wanted the same, I wouldn't need to come crawling to you because I'd be far, far richer than you'll ever be. But by all means, Constantine. If you're that basic and boring, I'm perfectly happy to lie back and think of England on my mother's behalf."

She didn't know why she'd said that. Molly had no desire whatsoever to trade her body for anything, particularly not when she already used it as a product—and as such, was keenly aware of the kind of slippery slope divorcing her body from her emotions could be. She was fully aware that there was a cottage industry of those who claimed to have had passionate affairs with her, and she liked that. The more people gossiped about her, telling each other and everyone else lies about all the scandalous things she was up to in her spare time, the less likely anyone was to notice that she did very few scandalous things at all.

But she also knew, because she was a grown woman who lived in the real world, that few things irritated men more than being laughed at. Obliquely or otherwise.

So she was totally unprepared for Constantine to throw back his glorious head and laugh himself.

And laugh. And laugh some more.

"Did I say something amusing?" she asked when he finally stopped. A bit peevishly, she could admit.

And then watched, her mouth dry, as Constantine rose in all his considerable glory from behind that dreadful desk.

She had nothing but terrible memories of this place. Which was no doubt precisely why Constantine, who had more houses than he had race cars and he had a fleet or five of those, had chosen this one for their meeting. It was likely purely for her benefit, so she could truly connect with the unutterably stupid teenager she'd been when she'd lived here. How she'd crept in and out of these deceptively welcoming rooms, painted in bright Mediterranean colors that made the sea and sun seem the brighter, trembling like a fawn every time she drew notice from anyone. Staff and Skalas alike.

This particular room had been where Demetrius had liked to exercise the worst of his power—and he'd had entirely too much power. He had loved nothing more than calling Molly in to stand before him, her heart pounding in her throat and her stomach in knots, while he shared with her exactly how embarrassing she'd been at whatever dinner had occurred the night before. How gauche and dull, when he'd expected so much more of her.

Constantine unfurling his magnificence before her while he stood in the very same spot where his father had stood before him was like…cognitive dissonance. Everything that had happened here had been dark. Even though she knew it had been typical Greek weather during those years, she always remembered it as if it had been dark and dreary, because inside her, it had. And then there was Constantine, who somehow seemed to blaze with a golden light when he should not have. Especially not now. But it had always been the same. He had all that Greek sunshine bottled up within him and everywhere he went, it was as if he lit up the world with every step he took.

It was annoying enough even when a person didn't know the truth about his wretched, twisted soul.

And here, of all places, it left her…shuddery.

"I think perhaps you're willfully misunderstanding me, Molly."

He sounded casual and almost offhand. To disguise his true intentions, as always. Accordingly, he was dressed like a businessman, instead of the more casual things she'd seen him in over the years. Not that she was looking, ever, but they were often in the same tabloids. His version of a business suit was always…rumpled. That was Constantine. Always slightly in disarray, so it was impossible not to look at him and imagine what bed he had just rolled out of. Or if he'd troubled himself to find a bed at all.

Stop shuddering, she ordered herself, and had to fight not to press her hand to her belly. It would do nothing to quell her internal reaction to him, but it would certainly give her away.

As he rounded the desk, lazy and languid and seeming not to move at all even as he did, she assured herself that it was not that she was uniquely susceptible to him. It didn't matter that he had pretended to be her friend or not. Or that he clearly was unhinged to have plotted out an elaborate revenge against her poor mother. Those things were factors, but not in the way her body reacted to him.

She couldn't help it if she was a woman and he was not just a man, but *him*.

It was a perfectly natural physical, chemical response.

Molly certainly didn't have to *act* on it.

"You and I are going to start a flaming, passionate affair," he told her, oh-so-casually, as if he had summoned her here to chat about the weather. "It is going to be very, very public. I regret to inform you that like most women who become entangled with me, you will likely lose yourself. Fall in love, find yourself shattered, etcetera. It happens all too often."

"I'm not Icarus and you're not the sun, Constantine," she snapped at him. "I'm aware that might come as a shock to you."

His eyes gleamed. "We shall see. In any case, when I tire of you and your infamous charms, such as they are, I will discard you. Rudely and unfeelingly, I have no doubt. Then it will be up to you what you do afterward. Will you crawl off into obscurity as you should have done a decade ago? Or will you return to take your place on the runway, though you will be forced to accept that everyone who looks at you will no longer see whatever fashions you might be hawking, but my castoffs? Only time will tell."

Her brain literally would not make sense of any of that, because it all hinged on an impossibility. "You mean this is some kind of act we're going to put on… Right? Because, in case you've forgotten, you hate me. Remember?"

"I can only speak for myself," he said, sounding lazy and faintly amazed that she was asking. "But I do not *act* when I make love. And I do not make love, Molly. I make war. In war, I regret to tell you, there can only be one victor."

She knew she should have laughed at that. At him. It should have been hilarious. If any other man had said such a thing in her presence, she would like as not have broken a rib laughing too hard. She would have raced out of the room, contacted every friend she'd ever made, and invited them to laugh at him, too.

But nothing about Constantine Skalas was funny. Because she believed him. He'd been at war all along, she had simply been too foolish to see it. And deep inside, where she had always and only melted for him, she knew he meant everything he'd just said.

And then some.

"Why would I ever agree to such a plan?" she managed to ask.

He smiled then, devil that he was, and it was heartbreaking. For he looked positively angelic. His eyes looked almost warm, as if he cared deeply about her—or anything—when she knew that was patently false.

"I cannot think of a single reason that you would." He shook his head, almost sorrowfully. "I would not, if I were in your place. But then, I would have left your mother to rot long ago."

"The way you've left yours?" she shot back at him.

And knew instantly that she'd made a huge mistake.

Constantine didn't blow up the way his father would have. He didn't throw something breakable across the room. He only studied her as if she were an experiment on a slide beneath a microscope— one he intended to dissect—while everything about him went still.

"Do not mention my mother again," he said quietly. So quietly it was very nearly a whisper, and every hair on Molly's body seemed to stand on end. "You will find that there are few topics off-limits to me. I'm not a man with any boundaries, and I mean that in every sense. But my mother is off-limits to you."

"I haven't agreed to do any of the things you

suggested," she pointed out with a great surge of
bravado she only wished she felt. "If I want to talk
about your mother and the simple facts about her
that every single person on earth knows—"

"I can't stop you, of course." He cut her off
in that same quiet manner that made her spine
hurt because she was standing so straight, so tall,
for fear that if she did not, he would see how she
shook. "But know this. Every time you mention
my mother, I will take it as an invitation to vent
my displeasure on yours."

And as ever, Molly felt that same sick rush of
love and shame, frustration and longing that char-
acterized her entire relationship with Isabel. If she
could only find a way not to love her mother, her
life would be infinitely simpler. If she could only
harden herself and stop caring what became of Isabel, she wouldn't be standing here right now. She
could have carried on living a life completely apart
from even the faintest hint of the Skalas family, as
had been her preference for years now.

But it didn't matter how many times her mother
called her from the middle of what she liked to call
her *little scrapes*. Or how many times Molly swore
she would be done, once and for all, cleaning up
all of Isabel's messes.

Oh, Moll, her mother would say in that rueful,
smoky voice of hers, *I've really done it this time.*

And despite the number of times she'd received

that call, or had grudgingly agreed to let Isabel stay with her until she *sorted it*, which she never did, Molly still loved her. Molly couldn't help but love her. That was the whole of the trouble right there.

"Right," she said now, in Skiathos and in grave danger as well she knew. She kept her tone brisk. "No talk of mothers and I get to be your mistress, not merely a one-off shag. Brilliant. But how does that work, exactly?"

"How do you think it works?" Constantine's head tilted slightly to one side. Molly had the distinct and unsettling notion that he was less a man in that moment, and instead, some kind of overly large predator more usually found in the nature documentaries she watched when she couldn't sleep on whatever airplane she was on, jetting off to another job. "Have you not spent many, many years as a mistress to this or that man of appropriate means? What few there are in that tax bracket, of course. I am told it is very difficult to afford you."

That was possibly meant to be a joke, as there was nothing on earth or in the heavens above that a Skalas couldn't buy. Twice.

Molly opened her mouth to disabuse him of any notion he might have been harboring that she'd flitted about adorning the arms of the unworthy and unappealing men who thought they deserved her, no matter what the gossips liked to claim. But she caught herself.

Because if this was really going to happen—a possibility she couldn't quite allow herself to contemplate too closely, because it was too much, and too dangerous on a personal level after all she'd done to climb out of the abyss of her teenage years here—it would suit her far better that he thought of her as her alter ego. Magda.

Magda had been a creation of necessity. Molly Payne, awkward and shy, could not possibly have done the things she had if left to her own blancmange devices. But Magda could do anything. Magda had no fear. She was bright and strong, and when Molly was pretending to be her, the world around her was limitless. And usually hers for the taking besides.

Constantine insisted on calling her Molly, no doubt to remind them both of the power he'd held over her way back when. But clearly, he also believed everything he had heard about Magda. That could only work to her benefit.

Because Magda would think absolutely nothing about launching herself headfirst into a passionate love affair with the devil himself. In point of fact, Magda would find the whole thing unutterably delicious. She would laugh uproariously at the idea that she would ever be diminished by such a liaison. Not Magda. All Magda ever did was glow.

Molly regarded him for moment, collecting herself. Or collecting Magda, as the case might be, because that had always been much easier.

"Every man has a different set of requirements for the trophies he collects," she said nonchalantly. "And naturally, when the trophy is me, there are different considerations at play. My career is demanding and it will not stop being demanding to please the man in my life. Or even to accommodate him. And, of course, there is no possibility that I will ever waft about, waiting on a man hand and foot as some men long for. I require neither money nor the euphemistic *help* that such situations are generally made for, suiting all parties. So you see, it is indeed difficult to afford me, but not in the way you mean."

Well done, she congratulated herself. *Maybe next you can open up a brothel and make yourself the madam, since you're such a believable whore. That will be a terrific use of your talents. For lying.*

"That may have been your experience in the past," Constantine told her, a certain gleam in his coffee-dark gaze that made goose bumps rise all over her skin. "But this will be different. Because again, Molly, you are not the trophy here. You are working off a debt. Meaning, you will be the one doing the work. Because mark my words, you will pay. Again and again, until I am satisfied."

She believed him.

But she also knew him. And the Constantine she'd known, even if she'd deeply misjudged his vengefulness, had always been a glutton for attention. Good or bad, whatever worked. Molly had spent years trying to understand why, when now that she thought about it in the context of Demetrius's old office, it made sense. His father only doled out positive reinforcement every once in a blue moon, and usually to Balthazar. It had never seemed to bother Constantine much, for he was perfectly content to receive his father's negative attention. Just as long as he received it. And certainly all the behavior she'd seen in a thousand tabloid magazines over the years told her the same story. She didn't need a degree in psychology to work that one out—especially when she'd had a taste of the same hard school that had made Constantine who he was.

The hold Constantine Skalas had over her was insurmountable. Because like it or not, Molly could not bear to see her mother suffer. She could beat herself up about that all she wished, but she doubted it would change.

She knew it wouldn't change, or it already would have, at some point or another over the past ten years. Molly had watched her mother fritter away the fortune that had been her divorce settlement. Then she had drained the fortune Molly had built, too.

Molly did not care to imagine how many times Constantine had indulged his vengeful streak on her in that time when she'd been so blissfully unaware that he was the puppeteer controlling the strings, but it hardly mattered now. Because Molly knew that she was the only stepsister he'd had. That meant she knew a whole lot more about him than the average silly starlet who got mixed up with the famously beautiful and sexually voracious Constantine Skalas, imagining he'd be some kind of a lark.

When what he was, in fact, was lethal. Emotionally lethal.

But she felt that she could ignore all the goose bumps and that sense of foreboding that kept shaking its way through her, because she had her own weapons. Knowing him was the key.

He had rounded the desk and was now looming about within reach, which made her feel far too edgy. She drifted over to one of the chairs that sat about for decorative purposes, as far she knew, for never in her memory had she ever dared sit when summoned into this room. But sit she did now, draping herself across the nearest chair, the very picture of boneless ennui.

"Very well," she murmured. She draped one long leg over the opposite knee, letting her wick-

edly high shoe dangle sullenly, and waved a languid hand.

"Very well?" echoed Constantine, and he
sounded…incredulous.

He moved to stand before her in all his rumpled male beauty that she knew she should have
found malevolent. But her body refused to get that
message. No matter how bored she tried to look,
inside, she found it hard not to shiver. And melt.
And shiver some more. Her breasts felt tight and
high, her belly was tied in a knot that pulsed, and
between her legs she was slick. Hot.

Desperate and aching.

You are a betrayer, she told herself sternly.

But what she did was *almost* shrug, then *almost* wave her hand, looking as deeply bored as it
was possible to look without falling asleep where
she sat.

"Very well then," she said, a little more slowly,
as if he was dim. And watched that incredulity
make his gaze narrow. She only sighed in response. "Let me know how you want me to do all
this debt repayment. Let me guess. You'll want a
sad, tawdry blow job here and now, because nothing says a man has power more than waving his
little head around and making beautiful women
genuflect before it. Or I know, maybe you want to
toss me over some of the furniture for that shag, so
it can be as dehumanizing as possible. I hear that's

how the garden-variety seducer prefers to pave his way into deeper and deeper levels of sociopathy. You tell me. I doubt I'll notice the difference between this and the average photo shoot, if I'm honest."

And Molly had almost convinced herself that she was that jaded. That it wasn't even the usual Magda act. That she dripped scorn like a fountain and in doing so, had made herself untouchable, like stone.

Constantine laughed. A dark sound that sunk deep into her bones, making her feel as if they might shiver out of her skin, all on their own. As if the black magic sound of it might render her... someone else entirely than who she'd thought she was when she'd come here today.

Someone she was not at all sure she wanted to meet.

"Oh no, my little *hetaira*," he murmured, his voice another dangerous spell, and the gleam in his gaze a weapon. "That is not how this is going to go."

And then, standing above her like a judge on high, he reached down and hauled Molly to her feet.

Then slammed his mouth to hers.

CHAPTER THREE

MOLLY BURST INTO FLAMES, then exploded, and that was only a hint of the kind of heat that Constantine's mouth on hers generated.

It was only the start.

Her hands came up of their own accord, fluttering near his shoulders when she had never *fluttered* a day in her life. He was so big all around her when she was used to towering over most men. His mouth was so *hot*. And he angled his jaw as his tongue swept hers, making her shiver out as well as in.

His kiss was slick, wicked and insidious, and almost unbearably good.

He kissed the way he did everything. Lazy, reckless, and underneath it all, a dark edge of that same danger she really should have heeded.

She could taste him. Smell him. His tongue was a temptation, his sensual mouth a seduction, and she could hardly make sense of all the sensations that stormed in her.

Molly was lost.

All the dreams she'd had of him when she was a girl. All the stories she'd told herself about what it might be like if ever he actually noticed her. All her wildest fantasies—this was better than any of that.

This was so good she wanted to cry. Strip off all her clothes here and now. Throw herself at him—

Which, she thought with something far too close to horror when he wrenched his mouth from hers, was going to make her plan for surviving this a little tricky.

She hated him in that moment.

Molly hated that satisfied, entirely too male expression on his beautiful face as he gazed down at her, his huge and unfairly hard hands wrapped around her upper arms to hold her in place. How a great boneless cat of a man like Constantine Skalas could somehow, magically, be as fit as if he worked his days away in the proverbial fields was an outrage. It was *unjust*, was what it was.

And meanwhile, she was absolutely certain that he knew full well the effect he had on her.

Her lips felt swollen. She could taste him on her tongue, something rich and heady that she was half-convinced had already gotten her drunk. He looked entirely too pleased with himself, so she was sure he not only knew all of that, but more, knew that her nipples had pinched tight with need while the core of her had gone molten.

Damn him.

"Kissing?" She called on all the acting she'd learned how to do to have the career she had, and to do it well. Every single time she'd had to contend with a horrible photographer, a grueling schedule, the usual condescending way women in her profession were treated, had been practice for this. And the faintly surprised but mostly bored tone she employed now. "Since when is there *kissing* when you're paying for it?"

Constantine's smile was a flash of white teeth, just this side of fangs. Or so she assumed when it hit her like a blow and made her feel tottery in her heels when she'd mastered stilettos back at age eighteen.

"I'm not interested in your ice queen act, Molly," he said, still smiling.

"What makes you think it's an act?" She tilted her head to one side and stood there woodenly, as if she had men's hands on her and their faces scant inches from hers every hour of the day. Which was not too far from the truth, though usually, at work, there was none of this spiky, brooding tension in the air. "I had a rough adolescence. My mother married a truly awful man and the blended family thing was hell on earth. But luckily enough, it cured me of feeling much of anything too deeply."

His smile took on that feral edge she remembered too well, though back then, she'd been foolish enough to mistake it for something else. Like empathy on his part. "I'm sure that's the story you like to tell, stepsister, but we both know it is not the truth."

"All right," she said, patronizing him. And making sure that he was fully aware that was what she was doing. "You know me better than I do. Got it."

Constantine…did something then, though she couldn't have said what it was. His hands were on her arms still, making her wish she'd worn some kind of sleeve to ward him off. Or to save herself, more like. That smile of his had settled into something worryingly *knowing* that she didn't like at all. And the gleam in his gaze was intense enough that it should have pierced her straight through. But then all of that changed, though she couldn't see how. It was as if he focused in on her, even more intently, and she lost her breath.

And he knew that, too.

"I think you'll find that there is no one on this earth who knows you better than I do, Molly. For your sins."

He released her arms and stepped back. And she was buffeted with contradictory sensations then. Relief. Loss.

And the heat in her rose all the while.

It did not wane, at all. Not even when it was clear that he was standing there, sizing her up the way they always did at work, as if she was a horse

at market. Molly felt lucky that she was used to it.
And more, that despite the reaction she was having, there was something soothing about being
treated like a mannequin that took direction. It
was her life's work, after all.

"The only things you know about me," she said,
fighting to keep her voice even, "are the things
I never should have told you when I was a silly
teenage girl who believed that Constantine Skalas
was actually my friend. But guess what? That girl
is gone. You got rid of her yourself."

"You learned a valuable lesson," he replied,
thrusting his hands into his pockets and giving her
a long, thorough, deceptively sleepy once-over that
made everything inside her prickle into high alert.
"It is an act of supreme foolishness to trust anyone.
Some don't learn this until it's too late. You learned
it while you were but a girl. You should thank me."

"Thank you." Her voice was acidic. "And how
proud you must have been to take it upon yourself
to teach such a harsh lesson to a lonely girl. Such
a humanitarian you are. I'm shocked you haven't
collected awards for your services to mankind."

His smile was an exercise in seductive menace.
"But we are not speaking of a hapless, awkward
teenage girl, the daughter of a grifter of a housekeeper who fancied herself a replacement mother.
As well as an actual mistress of the Skalas estates, rather than my father's tawdry affair that

he dressed up in legalities for reasons that died with him."

There wasn't much anyone could say about Isabel that Molly hadn't thought herself. But that didn't mean she liked hearing it. "Yes, my mother woke up one day and just *imagined herself* your stepmother. Nobody pursued her. Or married her. Or told her to do as she pleased with the estates and the stepsons and everything else because, Lord knows, *he* certainly didn't care either way."

"My father is dead and cannot account for his decisions." Constantine shrugged, a masterpiece of Mediterranean nonchalance. "And would not have anyway, even had he lived."

"Right. You expect me to believe that while he was alive you changed the habits of a lifetime and took him to task for his behavior?" Molly laughed, and then laughed a little harder when she saw how little he liked it. "I'd like to have seen *that*. You know full well that the only thing he cared less about than what my mother did with his money was you. He likely would have cut you out of his will for suggesting otherwise."

She thought she saw the hint of a clenched jaw, which she told herself was a win. But was it really? Because the way he was looking at her...

"I'm interested that you seem to think insulting my father—and me—is a good way to begin a debt repayment program."

"Is it an insult to speak the truth about a man we both knew?" Molly shrugged, aware that when she did it, it was less a study of carelessness and more a sharp little gesture of disdain. She'd practiced it for years. "I wouldn't even say that's any kind of insider take on the late, great Demetrius Skalas. He was a complete mystery to me while my mother was married to him. Anything else I might have gleaned about him is public information." She counted off on her fingers. "He was a terrible person. His sons are terrible people. That's not my opinion, that's just a couple of incontrovertible facts."

Constantine smiled, and she regretted, deeply, that once again she couldn't seem to control her mouth in his presence. *Damn* him.

"Here are some other facts," Constantine murmured, all dark undertone and that glinting thing in his bittersweet gaze. "You have a martyr complex, for I assume you must get some sort of pleasure out of sacrificing yourself for your mother at every turn. Or why would you do it, again and again? She is a grown woman, capable of handling her own life—except she need not trouble herself with such things, because you do it for her."

Molly assumed he wanted a response from her, so she only gazed back at him, mutely defiant.

He continued. "For all that you travel about the world, command top dollar for pouting at the camera, and have entertained more rumored lovers than photographers, you're a very, very lonely woman."

She would die if he saw any kind of reaction on her face. *Die.* And still it took everything she had to simply continue to stare back at him as if he hadn't done that thing he'd always done. Smile and then skewer her.

"I know this because I watched you, Molly," he said, his voice getting quieter. But she watched his eyes. And the way they gleamed, that dangerous gold. "Every year you get thinner. Your eyes go darker. You become more and more brittle. Do not mistake me, your beauty, certainly a surprise to any who saw you as a gawky sixteen-year-old, only grows. But you're not happy, are you?"

She continued to stare back at him, but once the silence stretched between them, she gave an over-the-top sort of start. "Oh, my bad, is this the part where I actually respond to the man who's *blackmailing* me? I thought this was all rhetorical."

"I know what you eat, how long you sleep, even what documentaries you like to watch," he told her quietly, his dark gaze all gold, telling her clearly that he was showing her his weapons even if she hadn't heard him. "I know what you do when you're without one of your command appearance parties to attend in whatever city you find yourself."

"Why, Constantine. I'm flattered."

"You walk," he said, with a certain soft menace. And that time, she doubted very much that she managed to conceal her reaction. And then knew she hadn't when his gaze lit with victory. "Around and around and around whatever city or town you happen to be in, and you're not taking in the sights, are you? You prefer to go at night, almost as if there are demons you're trying to put behind you. Your mother, perhaps?"

"Wrong again," she replied, holding his gaze as if none of this scared her. When it did. When *he* did in more ways than she ever planned to admit. "I've only ever known one demon, Constantine. And he is standing right in front of me."

"I know you," he said again, clearly relishing this moment. Clearly enjoying this. "And when I have you, and I will, I will have all of you. And if there's nothing left after I glut myself on all you have, all you are, maybe you can see how it feels to put yourself back together." His dark eyes blazed. "The way my mother tried to do after yours took her place."

Molly was back home in London by evening, feeling as jittery as if she'd existed on nothing but caffeine and cigarettes for three weeks—a lifestyle she'd given up in her first year of modeling, because that led nowhere good. And was unsustainable besides.

It was a rainy, cold, and foggy May evening,

and the shift in the weather from Skiathos to England's best plunged her instantly into a mood that was far too reminiscent of sixteen-year-old Molly. First plucked out of gray, miserable England and swept off to the dazzling coast of a Greek island, out of her depth in every possible way.

The sun had burned her skin a bright, feverishly painful red within an hour of her landing at the Skiathos airport. She should have known, even then, that it was only the first of many ways Greece would sear straight through her.

And when Isabel had finally left Demetrius and his power games, creeping back to England to lick her wounds and to hire a set of sharks to handle the divorce, Molly had felt the loss of all that terrible light and heat too keenly. It had felt like dying.

She felt the hint of that feeling again now, as her car bumped along the cobbled mews not far from Hyde Park and dropped her off at the Mews house she'd bought when her career first took off. A stone's throw from the Marble Arch, Hyde Park, and Oxford Street, her little house was a quiet retreat from the bustling, busy city all around her. It was also *hers*. All hers. She'd bought it with cash, filled with the naive hope that the one thing that was finally hers and only hers would stand as a symbol toward a bright future. The one she'd been determined to have, because she was sure she could make it different from the childhood she'd lived, the mistakes she and her mother had made in turn, and everything else she wanted to turn her back on.

Everything tainted by the Skalas family, in fact. And it had worked.

Her Mews house was a home, not an investment piece. It gave her four walls, three floors, and two lovely terraces' worth of peace. It was the only place on the planet where she could happily be herself. There were no pictures of Magda gracing the walls inside. There were no magazines. Inside, there were only the things she loved wholeheartedly. Books and art and other things she'd picked up in all the places she'd traveled. Bright colors and deep, soothing chairs and sofas, because every square inch of the place was meant for relaxation and recharging.

Out on the charming cobbled street as the car pulled away, Molly took a deep breath and let it go into the damp night. But the place still did its magic. Her shoulders lowered. That pounding in her chest settled. The knots in her belly eased... a little.

She let herself in the heavy door and heard the sound of music from the second level in what her real estate agent had loftily called her *reception room*. It was the heart of the little house. Kitchen on one end, a great hearth, French windows and a terrace over the cobblestones, and all the over-size, cozy things Molly had managed to make fit.

And since the last great implosion of her latest scheme, courtesy of Constantine Skalas, her mother, too.

Molly shrugged off the wrap she'd worn on the plane, hanging it near the door in her downstairs foyer. She kicked off her heels, flexing her toes against the polished wood floor as she padded up the stairs, absently reaching up to gather her hair, twist it back, then secure it in a thick ball on the top of her head. She walked up into the great room that had enough windows to make it bright and sunny on the days the weather wasn't foul, and she liked to sit out on her terrace and soak it in. And the clear nights, too. But tonight it was wet and cold, and anyway, even this magical little house of hers wasn't quite the oasis of calm when Isabel was around.

Her mother looked up as Molly walked into the room, looking flustered and determined all at once. "Darling. You're home at last. I've spent all day making the most *divine* pasta from scratch. As an offering."

"I can see that," Molly replied. The kitchen was a disaster. Pots and pans she didn't even know she owned were not only out, but half-filled with this or that, every single one of them noticeably dirty.

"Don't tell me you're not eating carbohydrates

tonight," Isabel continued airily. "Pasta is the least you can do for yourself after the day you must have had."

And though Molly opened her mouth to say that no, obviously she couldn't eat bowls of pasta, she stopped herself. Because, actually, pasta sounded absolutely perfect for the mood she was in. She didn't want anything to do with all the feelings swirling around inside her. Might as well eat them instead.

Still in the slinky dress she'd worn to Magda up the situation with Constantine, she didn't comment on the state of her kitchen. She simply set herself to the inevitable task that would fall to her anyway, of washing the dishes as her mother fluttered about putting the final touches to her homemade masterpiece.

By the time they sat down at the table near the side windows, Molly felt a bit better for having had the opportunity to lose herself a bit in the sheer drudgery of scrubbing and rinsing and drying, all better than thinking or feeling anything. It reminded her of long, long ago, when her mother had been a housekeeper in a grand house and she and Molly had lived in a small rented cottage in the village. On Isabel's days away she and Molly would cook up fanciful meals and then dress up to please themselves.

She'd spent so long trying to repress those years

in Greece, she too often forgot that she and Isabel had, in fact, had a whole life before the Skalas family had crashed into them and crushed them flat.

"I'm quite impressed, Mum," she said after her first, marvelous bite. "I know you can cook when you have a mind to, but I would have thought pasta from scratch was a bridge too far."

Isabel was still the beautiful woman she'd been when she'd caught Demetrius's eye in the stately old home where her family had been in service, in one form or another, since around about the Norman conquest. Beautiful and young, since she'd had Molly when she'd been seventeen—and had never named the father. *He knows where we are if he can be faffed*, she'd said dismissively. *No sense in chasing after a man if he doesn't want to be caught. There are always more.* That attitude hadn't made much sense to Molly back then, when she'd been the object of scorn and derision in the village herself, little though Isabel ever took notice. Now she understood Isabel's lack of concern. She was very, very pretty.

Too pretty to be a housekeeper, the tabloids had screamed when Demetrius had married her, then paraded her in front of the world.

He hadn't taken that from her, Molly thought with a rush of that same old love that got her into trouble. Nothing ever dimmed Isabel's spirits for long, and unlike many in her position, all of her looks were natural. No work.

At the moment, she looked rueful. "I'm not a total disaster, then," Isabel said with that self-awareness that always took Molly by surprise. "That's something."

"Of course you're not a disaster," she replied.

Isabel sat back in her chair, her bowl filled with pasta and aged parmesan steaming before her. "Go on then. Tell me what the damage is."

And Molly had intended to do exactly that. She had practiced fiery speeches on the plane ride home, each more bracing than the last. Hard truths were needed, she'd assured herself. It was high time she and Isabel *came to terms.*

It was always easier to fight with the people she loved in the abstract. Or the person she loved, to be more precise. Because it was only this one. Only and ever her beautiful, reckless mother, who for all her faults, loved Molly completely. Unconditionally. Even if that might not look the way Molly wished it would—like those long-ago fancy dress evenings, kitted out in costume jewels and pretending they were in Italy—it was real.

Molly knew that she could say anything to her mother. Isabel's guilt was a real thing. She had no qualm whatsoever about admitting fault, and apologizing, and taking it if Molly needed to shout at her.

But somehow, tonight, Molly felt that shouting at Isabel would be giving horrible Constantine Skalas exactly what he wanted.

I will need time to consider your charming proposal, she had told him with a regal disdain in that office.

Think of it less as a proposal and more as a lifeboat you do not deserve, he had replied, looking maddeningly handsome and inexcusably sure of himself. As if he already knew, as she did, that there was almost no way to get out of it and like it or not, she would be slinking back to him to do precisely as he commanded.

Still, she needed a bit of space, first. She needed to recalibrate. Because she'd expected that her temper would be involved, and she'd known deep down that what he would ask of her would feel unbearable, but what she hadn't expected was her response to him. That wildfire that raged in her still, and led to an insidious little voice inside wondering if really, it wouldn't be *too* bad, would it?

She'd wanted to rail at Isabel. It wasn't enough that Isabel had dragged her into the Skalases' harsh and cruel, glittering diamond-edge of a world back then, but now she was forced to return to it. To hand herself over to the architect of her first and greatest despair.

You are entirely too full of yourself, Constantine, she had told him. *No wonder you're so easily dismissed when you don't have a blackmail scheme in your back pocket.*

You are welcome to dismiss me, if you like, he had said in return. He'd even sounded encouraging. *My understanding is that you love that little house of yours in London. What a shame it would be if you were forced to sell it, to keep both you and your mother afloat in these uncertain times.* He had smiled when she glared at him. *Alternatively, you can return in two days' time, ready and willing to begin our torrid affair.*

She was still having trouble with that. An affair with Constantine when she'd barely survived a kiss? A *torrid* affair?

What would become of her?

"You're awfully quiet," Isabel said softly. She blew out a breath. "Is it that terrible?"

And Molly couldn't do it. She couldn't tear out another chunk of her mother's heart. Because that was the trouble with Isabel. Yes, she was impetuous and ambitious and had always had ideas far above her station. It was tempting to think of it as thoughtlessness, but it wasn't. It was that heart of hers. Big and foolish, and entirely too willing to think the best of terrible people.

Molly knew. She had the same one in her chest.

"No, Mum," she said, and summoned up a smile. "It's really not bad at all. Who could have guessed that in all these years since last we saw him, Constantine Skalas stumbled over conscience?"

"No one will believe that," her mother replied dryly. "Least of all me."

"Well, he has," Molly lied. "You can rest easy. He needs me to play a role, that's all."

Isabel frowned. "If the man needs an actress, he has the whole of the West End at his disposal, to say nothing of his liking for all of those bland little Hollywood types. Why would he need you?"

"He's far too well-known to go out and hire someone. This little spot of blackmail helps him save face, that's all."

Molly almost believed herself, she sounded so matter-of-fact. She smiled, then kept smiling, even though her mother's gaze was entirely too knowing.

Maybe, if she just kept smiling, she would convince herself, too.

"And who knows?" she asked merrily. "It might even be fun."

CHAPTER FOUR

IT WAS NOT until Molly reappeared at the house in Skiathos two days later that Constantine admitted to himself that he hadn't actually known if she was coming back at all.

And he was not suited to uncertainty. Nor used to it.

Not since Demetrius had died, at any rate, taking with him his cruel reversals, endless judgments, and what Constantine had always thought was a truly sadistic delight in the art of the sucker punch, both literal and figurative.

He had not missed any of that since he and Balthazar had buried the old man with all the pomp and circumstance of a monarch, according to his typically narcissistic instructions. Constantine had stood in the famed Metropolitan Cathedral in Athens that surely should have crumbled around him at his entrance, to say nothing of his father's many offenses against God and man, and had tried to look suitably grim and somber.

When all he'd been thinking was, *good riddance, old man.*

He did not appreciate the return to unpredictability. He resented any and all memories of his father as it was.

It was one more charge to lay at Molly's feet.

Constantine had been forced to sit about in that odd old house he'd never cared for, waiting. He had felt so worldly at twenty that he'd thought having to leave his admittedly nonchalant studies in London at all was a personal attack. He had especially disliked having to spend that first year's holidays marooned on this island with a new family he'd despised, as his father had demanded. This time around, as then, he passed the time by outlining all the ways he would take out his retribution on Molly and her mother. It was an exercise that had once filled him with what he'd assumed was joy. By a process of elimination.

Surely it should have done so again, especially given the fact that *this time*, he had a great deal more leverage. Yet as the two days he'd given Molly dragged by, he found himself far more invested in her return to Skiathos than he should have been.

Because it was only one of the options he had before him, as well he knew. He should have been equally invested in all of them. Forcing her to sell that charming little Mews house of hers would deliver a serious blow, for example. He knew that. He should have been moving on that angle while he waited.

The problem was that now, having seen her in person again, Constantine was far more interested in the angles that involved the flesh. Her flesh and his. He had always viewed sex as akin to the hotel buffets he'd observed in the properties he owned— readily available and very, very rarely worth the trouble. He had certainly never had to *convince* a woman to sleep with him.

In point of fact, he was far more often engaged in scraping lovers off, not obtaining them.

Yet Molly was different.

He told himself it was because of their history. Because of her déclassé mother and the fact they'd all been forced to share space—this space. That was what made her an obsession. That was why he sometimes felt haunted by her. And had for years.

But he had the taste of her in his mouth now and he couldn't seem to get past it.

And he had expected that Molly, in person, would prove the rule that photography was a very specific kind of magic. He'd expected her to look sallow. To have terrible skin, lank hair, or both. To make it clear, up close, that she had good bones but that all those pictures of her were simply make-believe.

Instead, he'd been astonished—and furious,

frankly—to discover that if anything, the camera was unkind to Molly Payne.

Because she was far more beautiful in person than she'd ever been on film.

Constantine had been tempted to throw away all his plotting, keep on kissing her, and to hell with their past.

Really, that alone should have had him calling off this whole thing and moving against Isabel a different way. Because clearly, he was unprepared for the reality of his former stepsister, and the fact that he didn't wish to accept that didn't make it any less true.

That he'd woken in the night, his body hard and aching for her, his head filled with intense images of the two of them together, had not helped.

He'd stood out on his balcony in the dark, too aware that he need not suffer through his own desire if he did not wish it. He could go down into Skiathos Town and have his choice of women to slake his lust. If he listened, he could almost hear the sound of the island's nightlife on the breeze. And it had been a very long time since he'd had to control his own desires, if ever. He was not certain he had ever waited for a specific woman in his life. There was never a need for specificity when the world was filled with so many options.

Go, he had ordered himself. *Get a woman and get a handle on this madness now.*

But he hadn't taken his own advice.

And he did not wish to acknowledge the sense of something far too close to relief he felt when his staff announced Molly's arrival. Precisely two minutes before her two days were up.

It wasn't *relief*, he told himself now. It was merely a well-earned pleasure that his plan was continuing as it should, particularly now she'd returned.

He did not have her shown into his father's wretched study this time. He had spent his morning dealing with any number of tedious business concerns and was now sitting out on one of the many terraces, taking in the sparkling blue of the cove below him. Still, he knew the moment she rounded the corner, taking the outside stair from the front of the house, draped in bougainvillea all the way. And this time, there was no click of high heels against the stones.

Constantine smiled, for he could only assume that meant the battle was on.

Sure enough, when Molly finally presented herself before him—clearly in no rush—she wore a black dress that had to be at least three sizes too large for her elegantly slender frame. Her long blond hair was pin straight and tucked behind her ears. She even wore trainers. She looked like what she was, a model dressing down, but if she was trying to make some kind of point about how unglamorous she was in the everyday, it was ruined by the simple fact that there was no disguising the simple perfection of her features.

A truth he had spent very little time acknowledging was that her features had always been perfect. She had been a distracting, arresting teenager, something he at twenty had noticed and then studiously ignored. Her mother's beauty had been softer, more accessible. *More common*, he would have said. And had.

All of Molly's features, taken separately, had seemed too bold or too full-on. Like that mouth of hers or her commanding height. Even back then, the way they'd all come together had always and only led to being found stunning, not pretty. For she was nothing so simple as *pretty*. She was nothing accessible or easy. Hers was a haunting beauty, and a shapeless black dress could do nothing at all to disguise it.

"I see you dressed up for this auspicious occasion," he drawled, lounging in his chair as if he had spent the morning here, lazing the day away. He imagined she probably thought he had, and as ever, it amused him to let people think the worst of him.

"I thought you would appreciate the mourning attire," she said, smiling. "It seemed appropriate."

"You have no idea how much." He was wearing his unofficial uniform when in the Greek islands, or forced aboard a yacht. Linen trousers that breathed in the heat and one of his favorite T-shirts, and he was aware that when he had not bothered to shave, as today, it made him look disreputable. All the better. "Have you come to mount more arguments? To see if you can somehow change my mind? You won't, but it might be entertaining to hear you out."

"What would I do?" she asked, widening her eyes a little, though he did not believe the innocent act for a moment. "Appeal to your better nature? Does such an animal exist?"

Constantine found himself grinning at that, which was not precisely how he had planned to conduct his great revenge. But what did it matter if they ended up in the same place? They would. He would see to it they did.

"Then dare I trust that you are here for the long haul?" he asked her, idly, as if whether or not she stayed was of little personal interest to him.

Because it should not have mattered.

"You already told me I have a martyr complex, Constantine." She held her arms out at her side, as if she anticipated a crucifixion. "Here I am, ready and willing to be burned all nice and crispy on the pyre of your choosing."

"I'm delighted to hear it."

He stared at her for a long moment, taking in the mulish set of her chin and the way her clavicle presented itself from the wide neck of the dress she wore, begging for his mouth.

Oh yes, this was happening.

Finally.

"I'll be honest with you, Constantine," she was saying, her voice bright enough that she might have been at a cocktail party instead of her own doom. "You don't look delighted. I would say rather that you look a little…dark."

"You have no idea, *hetaira*. But enough small talk." He settled back in his chair and let his smile go lazy. "Take off all your clothes."

And she was not so mulish suddenly. She did not precisely jolt in surprise, but he thought he saw the hint of it, quickly repressed. Her eyes, that arresting, arctic blue, deepened into something that almost matched the Aegean Sea stretched out behind her.

Almost.

"You don't waste any time, do you?" she asked, still staring back at him.

"I like to start as I aim to go on," he replied. "And, Molly. You are stalling."

He saw her gather herself, and he wondered if she would balk now. It wouldn't surprise him. After all, she was clearly a proud creature, or she could never speak to him the way that she did. Constantine, too, knew something of pride, and could not imagine any scenario in which he would subject himself to another's will in this way.

But even as that notion bloomed in him, he brushed it aside. They were nothing alike. He had no idea why he'd thought such a thing in the first place.

"And what happens if I can't go through with this?" Molly asked quietly.

"No one is forcing you," Constantine reminded her. He made a small show out of a shrug. "There is no gun to your head. You are not imprisoned here. The doors are open, the gate is unlocked, and you may leave whenever you wish."

"How generous." Her eyes glittered. "Yet if I do leave, you will ruin my mother. Possibly permanently. And who knows if you'll stop there. You might also take my house. Then make it difficult for me to work, I'm assuming. And probably, in the end, ruin me, too. Is that right? That has to be the goal or why bother?"

Constantine sighed as if pained. "It is a pity. But in life, there are consequences."

"This is how you sleep at night?"

He laughed. "Oh, *hetaira*, I have never had a night of troubled sleep in my life."

"Why would you? That requires a conscience."

"Now you're boring me." He shook his head. "Make your choice. Stay or go, as it please you.

But if you stay, you heard my instruction. I would suggest you follow it."

"What a lovely invitation," Molly said, through her teeth. "How can I possibly refuse?"

Neither one of them pointed out that, of course, she couldn't.

Then, with a notable surliness he almost applauded, because she made so little attempt to hide it, she toed off her trainers. One, then the next. Then, with the level of sensuality Constantine would expect to see in a doctor's surgery, she pulled off the dress, tossing it onto one of the chairs nearby. Then she stood there before him in nothing but a pair of thong panties.

God help him.

And he could see that she had shifted into her work mode, as he liked to call it. She'd become the other version of herself. Magda. Her gaze became haughtier, sharper. The way she stood changed—to encourage, not touching, but looking. A fierce stance that commanded attention. She was suddenly imperious as she stared at him, almost as if she was challenging him. Did he dare to come before her without a camera to begin worshipping her with its lens, as most did when they beheld her?

And why not? Molly was a masterpiece.

She was all long, elegant lines and surprising curves. Two perfect breasts sat high on her chest, the nipples tightening as he looked at them. If

Molly noticed, and Constantine was sure she did, she gave no sign.

Instead, Molly continued to hold his stare in that challenging manner of hers as she bent, stripped off her thong, and tossed it to the side as well.

Then she stood again, looking utterly at her ease. Her hands by her sides, her weight shifted to put her at her best advantage, and how could he not appreciate the view? He more than appreciated it.

"Well?" she asked, and not in the tone of one who had any doubts about what she was presenting.

"You have a very strange take on the idea of servitude," Constantine pointed out. "I find this amazing, given your mother's initial profession."

"Yes, cleaning a house is like brown eyes," Molly agreed, her tone like a lash. "Passed down generation after generation, by genetics. I was personally born with a broom in one hand."

"Here are the rules," Constantine said, ignoring that. "As you are well aware, this is the house where my father always insisted we live without a full staff. I assume because it gave him pleasure to make your mother do the housekeeping. I will not do the same."

"Whyever not? I was sweeping up before I could walk. A family trait."

"My assistant stays in the guesthouse and is rarely here in the main house. And never without advance warning. There are guards at the gate, as I'm sure you saw, but they do not venture within. I tell you this to forestall the inevitable argument you're going to attempt to have with me when I tell you that while we are here, unless I specifically tell you otherwise, you will be naked."

"Naked," Molly repeated. "I'll just be wandering about, draping myself on the furniture, naked. That doesn't sound hygienic."

"Do you have a medical issue that should be taken up with a doctor?" he asked, silk and menace and entirely too much delight. "Do I need to bring in a medical team?"

"I'm sadly all too healthy and not about to die from a stroke, which is a tragedy." She glared at him. "But in case you've forgotten, I sunburn very easily."

"That will not suit me at all," Constantine assured her. "But no need to fear." He nodded toward the table beside the chair where she'd tossed her clothes. "I brought you some sunscreen. Bring it to me, please. I'll apply it."

Then he watched, fascinated, as she looked from the tube of sunscreen to him, then back again, clearly fighting with herself.

He sat back and enjoyed the show.

And, if he was honest with himself, enjoyed the moment or two to pull himself together, because he had not quite anticipated the effect this would have on him.

Constantine had seen more beautiful women naked than he could begin to count, but this was different. She was different.

He was so hard that he ached. He *ached*. He wanted to throw all his years of careful planning aside and simply take her, as he knew he could. He had not imagined the way she'd responded to that kiss. He had not liked the way he had, come to that. He had meant it as a show, more than anything else. But somehow, what had started as an object lesson had turned into something else.

He was Constantine Skalas and he had spent the last two days reliving a bloody kiss, of all things. As if he was the gawky, awkward sixteen-year-old this time around. As if she had bewitched him, and that easily.

He would not allow it. He refused to allow the daughter of the unacceptable tart Isabel Payne, of all creatures, to affect him in this way. Or at all.

It was a physical reaction, that was all. She had made an entire career out of her beauty. She knew very well how to elicit the reactions she wanted. He should not be so surprised that he was susceptible to it. What man would not be?

Because naked, Molly was even more beautiful than she was draped in all the dramatic clothing she wore on this or that runway. Once again, he was struck by the stark, glorious lines of her body. A work of exquisite art, angles and curves together, creating a woman no one could deny was exquisite.

And now, for as long as he wanted her, she was his.

Molly came to her decision. He could see it on her face in the split second before she swiped up the tube of sunscreen with one hand, then closed the distance between them. With a challenging look on her face as she stood there, naked, as commanded.

"Come closer," he told her, the terrible wolf to the not-quite-a-lamb, and when she did, he grinned. He held out his hand for the sunscreen, then waited.

And watched his favorite enemy as she fought, then surrendered, right there before him.

The way Constantine intended to see she did over and over and over again, until there was little left of Molly Payne but shattered pieces, and all of them in his hand.

CHAPTER FIVE

MOLLY HAD NEVER been more grateful for her chosen profession.

Because if it weren't for all her years as a model, could she have handled this? Could she have presented herself, so matter-of-factly, wholly naked in front of a man?

Not just any man. But Constantine Skalas, who had long been a shadow over her life whether she admitted it or not.

She tried to tell herself that there was nothing particularly worthy of her notice here. It was another gig, that was all. And luckily enough, she was more than used to finding herself in states of undress with very little privacy. If she'd been at all prudish about her body, she wouldn't have lasted a month in the fashion industry. Much less a decade.

Constantine took the tube of sunscreen from her, and Molly told herself to pay no mind to the fact that she was now standing between his outstretched legs. He took a long, lazy survey of her body, and she supposed she ought to have been grateful that he'd chosen to seat himself at the fanciful table she'd been enamored of when she'd been here the first time. This particular table was basically a shelf that ran around the trunk of a large shade tree, making it possible to sit out on this particular terrace in the high heat of a Greek summer day and enjoy the cool breeze from the sea without broiling.

It made her wonder exactly how calculating Constantine really was. But even as she thought that, she had her answer, didn't she? For here he sat in the shade, demanding her nudity, a convenient tube of sunscreen at the ready.

Molly really ought to have been ashamed that even now, when she had returned to Greece to trade her body for money—dress it up or down as she pleased, that was what was happening, and not, for a change, in the name of high fashion— even in the midst of yet another terrible thing he was doing to her, she wanted to excuse him. To give him some other reason for doing what he did.

When she should know better. The man was pure evil. More, he was proud of it.

He finally raised his gaze to hers again, sensual and heavy-lidded and, as ever, richly intense. She did her best not to react and her reward was the hint of a knowing smile in one corner of his mouth. He lifted an idle hand, then circled one finger in the air before him, telling her without words to turn around.

Molly complied, executing a sharp, crisp turn that would have made art directors sigh with pleasure in at least five languages. She presented him with her back and then she stood still—another skill that the average person assumed anyone could do. When, in fact, real stillness for more than a moment was significantly more difficult than most lay people imagined.

Constantine was also still, and she resented that about him. That he could simply do things it took others a lifetime to learn. Much less execute on a whim.

After a while she had the sense of some kind of movement somewhere behind her and braced herself, but she heard nothing that sounded like Constantine about to strike. There was the sound of the sea in the distance and the waters of the cove against the shore. She could hear the breeze through the trees. She was aware of bees buzzing, birds conducting their officious business, and wind chimes, somewhere near.

All of it seemed entirely too bucolic and sweet when she'd woken up in a gray and wet London morning. Especially when Lucifer himself was here with her. She should have been able to smell the sulfur.

She waited, but nothing happened. Time stretched out. She held her breath, but still, nothing.

The Greek sun she would have sworn she hated filtered down through the branches of the tree above her, yet because it provided her with a canopy, it felt like nothing so much as a kiss. And slowly, against her will, she began to feel the inherent sensuality of what she was doing. Standing there, letting the breeze caress her while the sunshine licked all over her, soft and sweet. There was salt in the air, and the scent of something sweet that she assumed must be flowers, and she was sorely tempted to close her eyes and drift off…

But it was as if he knew. As if he could tell. Because the very moment she contemplated surrendering to this unusual moment she found herself in, he touched her.

It was torture in an instant. An exquisite, glorious torture.

And Molly had no idea why he'd turned her around so he couldn't monitor her expressions, because she was sure he would have seen far too much if he had. She felt her mouth drop open. Her eyes went wide. It took everything she had to keep her hands at her side, instead of letting them rise to cover her mouth. Her face. To do *something*.

Because Constantine was doing something so prosaic it should hardly have registered.

And yet.

His hands were big, faintly calloused from she knew not what, and slick with sunscreen lotion.

And it turned out that the most debauched and pointless man in the history of Greece was very, very detail oriented when it suited him.

He started at her hips, smoothing his hands to the small of her back, then all over her bottom, making sure to cover each curve. Then he slicked his way, ever so carefully, over her exposed inner thighs, down the backs of her legs, all the way along her calves to her feet, then up again.

Constantine said nothing while he did this. When he needed more sunscreen, his hands disappeared but always returned. The lotion was cool against her skin, but his hands were hot. Or she was hot. It was all *too hot*.

At some point he stood, and it took everything Molly had to keep from collapsing into a too-warm, coconut-scented puddle at his feet. Or even to keep her eyes open, because they drooped to half-mast as he rubbed lotion up the length of her spine. Then over each of her shoulder blades, then down the sides of her body, grazing her breasts at each side. But only grazing them, and then, as if he didn't notice, paying close attention to the backs of her arms.

"Lift up your hair," he murmured, though she did not mistake it for anything less than another command.

And in any case, she would have done anything he asked. Anything at all to keep his hands moving all over her like this, spreading heat and warmth inside and out and making her rethink her historic dislike of sunlight.

That was what it felt like. As if Constantine was sunshine and more, he was rubbing it straight into her bones.

"Turn around," he ordered her after a time, his voice gruff, and she didn't even think about it. There was no bracing herself now. No desperately trying to lock herself away somewhere inside her own head.

Perish the thought. All she could think about was more of that sunshine.

She turned again, and then everything seemed to ratchet up to such a high intensity that on some level, she was sure she had to be dreaming this.

Though she had never known a dream to be so tactile.

Constantine sat back down on the chair before her, picking up one of her feet and resting it on his broad, hard thigh. She had the strange notion that in this position, despite her nudity and all that was splayed before him, she should have felt regal, superior. Because she was not missish about being looked at, by any stretch of the imagination. He was below her, and surely she should have reveled in that.

But the truth was, she felt as if she might as well have been laid out before him on the ground, shuddering and boneless. She felt like a sacrifice. Yet for the first time in her life, she found herself questioning what that word really meant.

She had always used it in a passive-aggressive sort of way, particularly when it involved her mother and her *scrapes*. The sorts of angry sacrifices that a person made out of obligation, for example, meaning annoyances. Some larger than others but still, only annoyances.

But this man, this devil there before her, was running his hands up her slender calf, his attention seemingly so fixed on what he was doing that it made her feel hollowed out with a kind of shivering within.

And Molly found herself contemplating the notion of *sacrifice* in a new light. Everyone had seen those movies of girls dragged screaming to terrible deaths in the clutches of horrible monsters that heroes would then ride in to vanquish. *But what about the other girls?* she asked herself then, almost dreamily.

The ones who woke in the night, hot and desperate to wear a crown of flowers and a white dress. The ones who felt their very cores run hot at the notion of walking, of their own volition, away from the lights of the village, into the dark. The ones who shivered in delight at the idea of surrendering themselves wholeheartedly to the monster who waited there.

Why didn't they get any songs or myths? Why did no one tell their stories?

But she already knew the answer. No one mourned the girls who flirted with their own disasters. Mourning was for the good girls, the ones who behaved properly on the way to their deaths. All this time, Molly had been certain she was good.

But Constantine's hands taught her otherwise.

He did not look up at her, almost as if her reaction to what he was doing was incidental to him. And for some reason that made everything… tighter and hotter and wilder, until she felt molten straight through.

He is preparing your body for his pleasure, a voice inside her that sounded far too much like her own whispered then.

Molly should have been horrified. And yet she…was not.

She would not describe the breath she couldn't catch, or the way her nipples stood proud, or even that slickness between her legs that she was half-terrified and half-hopeful he would see as…horrified.

If he noticed her obvious arousal, he ignored it, moving with a certain briskness up the outside of her thighs. Then over her mound, ignoring the way she jolted as he made sure to rub lotion to cover all she kept bare, save for a tiny strip. Surely now he would shift everything over into a sexual place. Surely now he would make some kind of claim.

But instead, he sat forward. And took another age to move his slick palms over her belly, below and then above her navel. Eventually he made his way to her rib cage, where he climbed the length of her torso as if he could do so all day, and only stopped when he reached the under slope of her breasts.

Now her breath was coming in shallow little pants, and Molly should have been ashamed. Deeply ashamed. She should have held her breath until she passed out rather than show him how he affected her.

But it was as if her body was going to do as it wished. Or maybe he was simply that talented, even when it was something as small and seemingly nonsexual as the application of sunscreen.

It had never crossed Molly's mind that the man might actually have earned his reputation.

Constantine took his time putting more lotion on his hands, and then he moved again, standing once more so he could slick his hard palms over her breasts.

And then…he played with her.

Either that, or he was under the impression it took a remarkable level of detailed touching and caressing to protect her breasts from the sun. Not that Molly could really remember the sun or her usual aversion to it at this point or the world they both lived in.

There was only Constantine. There was only his touch.

He massaged her breasts with his palms, teasing her nipples into even stiffer points. Until she could do nothing but arch her back, let her head fall as it would, and press herself into his hands.

She'd never felt anything so delicious her life.

And somehow, without any idea how it happened, Molly found herself closer to Constantine. Had he pulled her there? Or had she simply drifted there of her own accord until she might as well have been in his arms.

Then his thigh was between hers and she found herself pressing the place she ached the most against his brutally hard, deliciously tough thigh. Then rocking herself there, lost in the rhythm of his hands on her breasts and her own movement on his thigh.

And then everything was slick heat and astonishment, and that coiling, shuddering, shimmering tension inside of her.

In the distance, or at her ear, she heard his gruff, dark voice muttering something she didn't understand. Greek, maybe. Or another incantation. It was too hard to tell.

And then she came apart.

Molly was a thousand shards of glass and still she came apart. Still the shattering went on and on.

She was dimly aware that she was still riding his thigh, that his palms were still working a rough magic against her nipples. And the connection between those two things was so intense, such a bright and impossible shine, that she felt as if all that light and wild heat was inside her. Then shattering outwards like all of that glass.

And then, for a time, she knew nothing at all.

It was only when she felt his hands on her shoulders, turning her and then guiding her down into the chair he vacated, that what she'd let happen here impressed itself upon her.

What she'd let happen and worse, what she'd done.

It took one breath, and then the shock of that realization hit her. Hard.

And right behind it came a wallop of shame. Liberally infused with the kind of self-recrimination she had last felt quite this keenly right here in Skiathos. And back then, she had never been naked in this man's presence, much less flung herself into his hands with so much heedless abandon.

Had she really been thinking about happy maidens scampering up mountainsides to fling themselves, breasts first, at the nearest scary thing they found?

It cost her more than she wanted to consider to

lift her gaze again, then to do her best to regard him coolly. Because it was all she could do.

And he was waiting.

"You come so prettily," Constantine told her, standing there before her with a little half smile on his perfect mouth and the glittering roar of heat in his gaze. "I hope you enjoyed a little taste of what awaits us on this little journey of ours. And the next time, Molly, you will have to beg me for your release."

"I think I can promise you that will never happen," she said, scraping up a truly miraculous tone of voice considering what was happening inside her, all scorn and haughty amusement.

But it was lost on him. All he did was let that half smile grow a bit deeper.

"Don't make promises you cannot keep, *hetaira*," he advised her in a low voice. "You will not like how I correct a broken promise, I assure you."

She could see that he was aroused himself. Yet he seemed to disregard it. To not even notice it, somehow, when she had always been under the impression that Constantine Skalas, above all men, was ruled entirely by that impressive length she could see pressed against his trousers.

Yet all he did was indicate the tube of sunscreen, still with that smile.

"Don't forget your face and neck," he said.

"You're already quite red. Though I do not think it is sunburn. Yet."

And then, to her astonishment—and what she would not have admitted was something far more complex than that, and a whole lot closer to disappointment—he simply turned and left her there.

She sat there, in the shade of that tree, for a long, long time.

And then longer still, as there was no getting past what had happened. What she had not only allowed, but had obviously reveled in.

Eventually, she took his advice and put sunscreen on her face and neck. Then sat there, certain that he must have been watching her, or waiting for her to…do something. It would no doubt indicate what was next on the naked blackmail menu for the day.

The shadows changed, yet Constantine did not reappear.

So even though she would have happily put it off longer if she could, Molly had no choice but to stand up, face the house behind her that she still hadn't gone inside this time, and then actually walk in of her own volition.

The house already made her feel vulnerable, and she shivered as she stepped inside, and not because of the temperature. She could see ghosts of her younger self everywhere she looked, and having to walk through these rooms literally naked, stripped down and vulnerable, did not help. She padded through the various living areas, trying not to see her memories play out before her, but there was no sign of Constantine.

Gritting her teeth, she moved on, making her way back to that dreadful study once more. But he wasn't there, either.

Eventually, she found him in the grand master suite that was its own wing of the house. She had not, obviously, spent much time here, as it was Demetrius's domain. And woe betide anyone who went somewhere he did not wish them to go. She had only vague memories of the way the suite was set out, with a sitting room here, a media center there. She told herself it was pleasant, by contrast, to walk through rooms with no ghosts at all.

But there was Constantine, and he was something far worse than a ghost. He was stood out on yet another balcony, his gaze on the sea beyond, speaking in impatient Greek into his mobile.

And yet somehow, Molly knew that he was perfectly aware of the very second she stepped out behind him. If not before.

He gave no indication that he cared either way if she was there, but she knew that he did. She just knew.

Constantine finished his conversation, and not particularly quickly, then turned, shoving his mobile in his pocket as he faced her. And she was struck—again—by his wholly unfair beauty. He was too masculine, too sexual, and yet somehow fitted perfectly here, where centuries back he should have been a god.

First monsters, now gods. She was losing it.

"You are lucky you did not attempt to defy me and dress," he said, though he sounded sorrowful. "I was so certain you would."

"Maybe you don't know me as well as you think," she replied loftily, and would keep to herself that new stab of self-recrimination. Because it hadn't even occurred to her to put her clothes on. What did that say about her?

Nothing good, she replied to herself. Nothing that wasn't more monsters and gods and willing sacrifices.

"I have a number of calls I must take today," Constantine told her, his dark gaze moving over her and making her feel as if he was still touching her. "I trust you can amuse yourself without supervision?"

"Am I allowed to amuse myself?"

His gaze gleamed at her dry tone. "In any way you like, save one. I already told you that your pleasure is at my command. And only when you beg me, Molly. I meant it."

She wanted to shake apart again, into a thousand new pieces because of that. And she was sure that he could see how close she came to doing it.

Instead, Molly pressed her bare feet into the smooth stone below, ordering herself to breathe. To remain calm. To use all the lessons she'd learned over time here. Among them, to stand about wearing or not wearing all manner of strange things while others stared at her.

Pretend this is a job, she told herself. *Because it is.*

"I don't think you need to worry about me running off to pleasure myself at the slightest provocation," she managed to say, just this side of withering. "I realize this may come as a surprise, but some of us are not quite so obsessed with endless sexual exploits as others."

"You could have fooled me."

That voice of his was dark like silk, and it curled in her like a threat.

She thought she should refute that. Fight him. Stand up for herself, for God's sake.

But Constantine only smiled. "You will stay in your old bedroom, naturally."

"Naturally," she repeated. Because that would be more torture, wouldn't it? "How appropriate."

His eyes brightened. "I saw that you brought only one small bag. I brought it in, but you will not need even that. If I wish you to dress, I will provide whatever it is I think you ought to wear.

Nightly, we will have dinner and you will wear whatever is left on your bed. And nothing else. Do you understand me?"

"With perfect clarity," she said. After all, her entire adult life had been about being *someone's* life-size dress-up doll. Why not his?

"Wonderful." The way he looked at her was predatory, though he did not move from the rail behind him. As if he was letting her know he could have. As if he was making sure she knew that everything that happened—or didn't happen—was entirely of his choosing. "Off you go then, Molly."

But she didn't move. She found herself scowling at him instead. "I have to say, I really thought the naked sex object thing would be a lot more about the shagging and a whole lot less about the endless mind games."

Constantine laughed, throwing his beautiful head back and making the Greek sky dim a bit behind him. "What would be the fun in that?"

"I rather thought the forced shag was the point. And the fun, from some perspectives."

"Oh, Molly. You've read this situation entirely wrong." Constantine leaned back against the balcony railing, regarding her with more of that deep male satisfaction that made her feel as if the ground beneath her feet was not stable at all. "I have no intention of forcing you to do anything."

"Except making me come here, then forcing me

to prance around naked for your entertainment, you mean."

That smile of his was…confronting. "I don't recall kidnapping you to get you here. Or tearing off your clothes. Or, for that matter, forcing you to orgasm while engaged in so prosaic a task as simple sun protection."

She felt herself flush, and there was no stopping that. "No, of course not. But persuasion is just a pretty word for force, isn't it?"

"It's a completely different word," Constantine said dryly. "And besides, I think the word that is the most germane to our situation is *consequences*. You don't like the consequences of some of your choices, that is all."

"I don't like the consequences of any of my choices," she retorted. And thought, *Or my mother's.*

"Such is life, *hetaira*. And someday, I have no doubt, you will dine out on all the stories of my wickedness. What a monster I am, how terrible, and so on. But between you and me, here and now, let us be clear. I have always given you choices. You always will have choices. And where there is choice, I think you'll find, there is no force."

She laughed at that. In disbelief. "Says the man with a sword hanging over my head."

"But therein lies the truth you're so desperate not to face," he replied, with quiet intensity. "That is not my sword. It is yours. By any estimation, you should never have had any money troubles again. And yet here you find yourself, naked before me, because of the choices you made long before you had the faintest idea what was waiting for you here. Blame me all you like. I'm used to it." He shrugged, the very picture of unconcern. "But when you're alone, Molly, and can look at yourself honestly, if you dare—remember. Blame yourself first."

And then he turned his back to her, leaving her to stew in his words for far too long. Before she slunk off inside…to do just about anything but look at herself in a mirror, honestly or not.

Because Molly already knew she would not like what she saw.

CHAPTER SIX

"I BEG YOUR PARDON." His brother Balthazar's voice was bright with amusement, and Constantine could practically see the look on his face, even though he was holed up far away on a private island down where the Aegean flirted with the bigger Mediterranean. He and the woman who was the daughter of the man who had destroyed their mother who Balthazar had married and impregnated, though not in that order. "Did you say Molly Payne? Our Molly Payne?"

"Perhaps you know her better as Magda," Constantine murmured. "Ridiculous as the name might be, and much as it pains me to admit it, she is universally known."

Balthazar laughed, which was a strange, new thing he did since his wedding. When, by rights, his marriage should have been as cold as the revenge he had always intended to wreak on his bride's family. Constantine could not get used to a lighter side of his grim older brother. It was… disconcerting.

"I don't know her at all, brother," Balthazar said. "No matter what name she uses. Because she was our stepsister for approximately five minutes and then I promptly forgot her."

"I did not."

The inadequacy of that statement clung to Constantine as the silence dragged out between Balthazar and him. Inadequacy and the fact that while he'd expected his fascination with Molly to wane after ten days in her constant company here in Skiathos, it had not.

And that, too, was putting it mildly.

His brother didn't have to know that. Just as Balthazar didn't need to know that Molly was currently dozing in a sun lounger that she'd pulled up beneath one of the umbrellas near the pool that was cut into the cliff below from the house, making its own level in the steep hill. Or that Molly came to him in the mornings, always naked and defiant, and he made sure to put the sunscreen all over her skin—though there was, sadly, no repeat of her ecstatic first reaction to his touch.

Was she fighting the simmering, greedy thing between them as hard as he was?

And did she understand that what he was doing was getting her not only used to his touch, but dependent on it—so that when she begged him for her release, as he knew she would, she would mean it?

Because sometimes that was all he thought about. Another thing he did not intend to share with his brother.

From his vantage point on the balcony off the master bedroom, he could see her where she lay. He could see how she glowed. She was stretched out on the lounger with a book in one hand and not a stitch on, which she had taken to as if it had been her idea in the first place. She wafted about the estate in the same manner, often frowning at him as if it was bizarre that he was actually wearing clothes.

He hadn't expected that his nudity decree would humble her—she was a woman who was not in the least ashamed of her body, and he liked that. It made her all the more beautiful. But he had expected some pushback, and there was none.

Her own way of fighting back, he supposed.

Constantine wanted her. Badly.

But the waiting only made the wanting better. And it would make her inevitable destruction better, too. Or so he kept telling himself.

"I wouldn't have mentioned Molly Payne at all," Constantine said into his mobile. "But she and I are undergoing a small negotiation that is taking more time than expected. I didn't want you to worry unduly if you heard mention that I wasn't in the office."

He ran the Skalas & Sons operation from their London base, but he traveled so much under usual circumstances that it was not as difficult as it might have been to handle his office from afar. And besides, there were so few members of his staff who understood that he was in no way the character he played for the world. He liked it that way.

But his brother was a different story.

"I did not realize that I was your keeper," Balthazar said, sounding amused when he was usually anything but. "Or your boss."

Constantine knew that most of the world was convinced the Skalas brothers hated each other. They had split the company after Demetrius's death—in the sense of their responsibilities, though too many people seemed convinced it had been a civil war. Balthazar spent most of his time in New York, Constantine in London. And because each one of them had chosen his own city and headquarters, and saw no reason to live in each other's pockets, this was seen as evidence of their undying loathing for each other.

Neither one of them had ever bothered to set the record straight.

The truth was far less interesting. They had grown up under the foot of a cruel man who'd pitted them against each other. They had not learned how to be close. Neither one of them, therefore, had ever craved it.

And yet, when Balthazar had chosen to marry his enemy's daughter, a move Constantine grudgingly admired as truly leaning into the long game when it came to revenge, Constantine had stood as witness. He had taken his place at his brother's side in the traditional role of *koumbaro* at the wedding and had been fascinated to discover that his always cold, always business-minded brother was far more emotionally involved with his pregnant new wife than Constantine had expected.

More than he'd thought was even possible for a Skalas, for that matter.

And he had found that while he had not known how to be close to Balthazar growing up, or if such a thing was wise with a father who sought always to crush them both—using whatever weapons came to hand—it seemed less a mystery now that they were grown men. He could simply be a brother. Just as Balthazar could in return.

Though it was easier to think such things and far more difficult to know what to do when opportunities arose to actually *be* brotherly in the way others, as far as he was aware, simply knew how to do since birth.

He found himself scowling down at Molly's beautiful form, laid out for his pleasure. And was too aware that Balthazar was perhaps the one man alive who would fully understand what he was about here. But that didn't mean Constantine knew how to go about telling him.

Money was easier. It was either made or lost. The numbers never lied.

They also never had *opinions*.

"I ran into Isabel at a charity thing some years back," Balthazar said, sounding nonchalant and conversational. Two things he had never been before his wedding. Constantine did not know whether to applaud or ask if Balthazar was feeling well. "She seemed far less of a gorgon than I recalled, it must be said."

"You are mistaken," Constantine bit off, staring at the gorgon's daughter. "She remains every bit the horror show she was then. Did you forget what she did?"

"I'll never forget what she *represented*," Balthazar said, with a not particularly subtle inflection on that last word. "But what did she *do*, really, except marry a man neither one of us liked much either?"

Constantine took that as an opportunity to steer the conversation away from the thorny topic of Isabel Payne, but he was still brooding about it when he and his brother ended the call.

And he continued to brood about it until dinner that night with Molly.

Because he liked her to dress in the evenings, he also allowed his staff in then. He had his cook prepare them the kind of meals he always preferred when he was by the sea. Light and fresh, assembling local ingredients and letting the dishes they ate look as colorful as the table they ate them on.

Tonight he waited for her on the low terrace, the one set even further down the cliffside than the pool. It was accessible only by a winding path, meandering this way and that, with nothing but the sea there below. At night it was lit by lanterns, all of them making little halos against the hill when he looked back up toward the house.

How had he failed to notice how beautiful it was here when he was younger?

But then, he knew. Every moment in this house had been a trial, and when he'd stormed off to Skiathos Town in the evenings, his focus had been on oblivion, not taking in the sights. And he didn't like to think about what his brother had said. He didn't want to ask himself what Isabel or her daughter had actually *done*.

They had been here. That was enough.

As always, he heard her coming a few moments later. And was perhaps too grateful to turn from his thoughts to watch Molly as she moved in and out of the halos strewn across her path. Then stepped onto the terrace that had lanterns everywhere, casting her in a golden glow that seemed to beat back the night sky.

For glow she did. Still. Perhaps always.

Her blond hair swirled all around her and the dress he had chosen for the evening was a splash of a deep blue that made her look almost otherworldly.

"Your dress-up doll is reporting for duty," Molly said. Then executed a sharp pirouette, swirling around before him in a manner he knew she meant to be mocking.

But he did not feel in the least bit mocked. Because the way this particular dress clung to her was a revelation. The fabric clung and swung, both calling attention to and yet concealing everything at the same time.

Constantine had discovered that the more she was dressed or undressed according to his whim, the more possessive he became. And he enjoyed knowing that she wore nothing but the dress, as he had requested.

As if he might, at any moment, have his hands all over her. He liked her to spend a lot of time, every day, thinking about that possibility.

He knew he did.

"I apologize that my sartorial selections do not live up to those of a woman renowned the world over for her style," he said dryly. "Which, as far as I can tell, involves wearing extraordinarily ugly things as a measure of defiance."

"You're not wrong," Molly agreed. She drifted closer to him and accepted the glass of wine he handed her. "But fashion is a self-conscious art by its very nature. Style is innate."

"Now you sound like one of those dreadful magazines. I thought you were more often seen draped across their covers."

Molly took a sip of her wine and, not for the first time, he was struck by her total lack of self-consciousness. She was disarming, this stunning woman who should have been prostrate in her room, weeping at the cruelty being visited upon her here. Instead, she seemed effortlessly charming—as she had been each and every one of the past ten days.

As a strategy, he was forced to admire it. Because she chose to engage with Constantine as if he was her host. Not her jailer.

When she was naked, it was easy to remember their actual roles here. But these dinners blurred the lines. They made him almost forget why they were really here—and he knew he couldn't allow that. He should put a stop to any part of this that did not serve his vengeance.

But though he told himself the same thing every night, he kept on with these dinners anyway.

He chose not to ask himself why.

Molly was studying him, her gaze cool but not unpleasant. It was clearly a part of her charm offensive—and he assured himself he was merely learning how she operated. Her weaknesses and fragile spots. Her surprisingly effective weapons.

"When you wake up of a morning," she said, "I doubt very much that you preen about in front of your mirror until you have achieved exactly the right level of casual chic. Mixed liberally with contempt at the very notion of casual chic, obviously. I think you likely…just get dressed."

"I pay other people to worry about my wardrobe," he replied. And smiled. "I already know I will look good in it, after all."

She lifted her glass in a mocking toast. "There you have it. Innate style. If you were fashion conscious, there would be more preening."

"You can't possibly be suggesting that you pay absolutely no mind to what you wear," he objected, mildly enough. "When you might happen to find yourself on a red carpet at any moment."

Her blue eyes looked something like merry. "No, of course not. What I'm saying is if I chose to wear a garbage bag to a red carpet, I would do it with such élan that garbage bags might very well become the rage afterward. That's style."

Constantine looked down at her and couldn't shift the same brooding mood he'd been in since his conversation with Balthazar.

"You're not the girl who lived here all those years ago," he said, in an abrupt growl. "Sometimes it's hard to imagine you could possibly be one and the same."

Her expression changed. And he had a quick,

uncomfortable bolt of recognition at the sight, because it was instantly clear to him that she was acting a part. The charming, artless version of her was a role. Perhaps it really was a part of her, too, but it was a part she used for her own devices. Why did Constantine find it so difficult to remember that she could not possibly have scaled the heights she had were she not capable of working a room? Just as he was.

That did not sit well. At all.

"Did you expect me to be sixteen, then?" she asked quietly. She gazed at him with those sharp eyes of hers, and Constantine suddenly felt exposed. The lantern light washing all over him didn't help. Her mouth curved. "Oh. You did. Let me guess how you thought *that* would look. You expected that there would be weeping. Maybe even a tantrum or two, since I was always accused of throwing those, though I never did. You expected me to turn bright red every time you deigned to look at me directly. And best of all, pick up where we left off, with me whispering my secrets into your faithless ear so you could use them against me."

That was as good a description of what had happened between them as any, Constantine knew. So why did he dislike it so intensely?

"If I'd wished for you to be sixteen again, I would hardly insist on your nudity," he pointed out. "It would muddy the retroactive teenage waters, don't you think?"

"Constantine." And Molly shook her head at him as if she'd expected better. "How could you possibly imagine that the same approach would work on me twice?"

"I am only pointing out that I thought there were only the three versions of you. That sixteen-year-old girl, you, and the role you play as Magda. I had no idea how many *other* versions of you there were."

"Maybe there's only one version," she replied, her cool blue gaze somehow filling him with fire. "Maybe you're the one who splintered into a hundred pieces, so long ago you think everyone else did the same."

"I am not the one with an alter ego, *Magda*," he said, with a laugh.

But she only smiled.

And then the food arrived, thankfully, before he could chase down whatever he saw in that gaze of hers that left him feeling… Edgy.

They ate in the lantern light. Perfectly grilled fish, local delicacies, and a few of Constantine's favorite forms of comfort food. Spanakopita. Saganaki. Honey-drenched sweets and strong coffee to finish. Far below, the sea threw itself at the cliffs and up above, the Greek summer sky put on a show as the stars beamed down.

And it had been ten days, yet Constantine—
who had long regarded himself as wholly irresistible to women, because he had yet to meet one who
had not said so herself—was no closer to demol-
ishing *this* woman than he had been before she'd
arrived on the island.

That was the trouble, he told himself. That was
why he did not feel quite himself. She was prov-
ing to be far harder to crack than he'd anticipated.

"How did you get into modeling in the first
place?" he asked.

Her gaze flicked to him, looking something
like amused. "Small talk? Really? I was wandering around your house today, naked from head to
toe, and you think *small talk* is the appropriate
response?"

"Is it that you cannot answer the question or
that you do not wish to?" was his cool response.

She shrugged, managing to make even that
a kind of pointed blade. "A modeling agent approached me on the Tube. I was eighteen and foolish enough to go around to the address on the card
he gave me. That's it. That's the story. It was all
fairly cut and dried, I'm afraid."

"But you must connect the dots for me." Constantine toyed with the stem of his wineglass.
"Because the girl who left Skiathos would never
have imagined that anyone could consider her
modeling material."

He did not know what he liked about the arctic blast he got from her then. Only that he did.

"You saw to that, didn't you?"

"I saw to it?" He sat back in his chair, taking his wine with him. "I'm guilty of a great many things, Molly, but I do not recall putting together a campaign against your... What is it you accuse me of? Your self-confidence?"

"But of course you did," she replied, with a certain simplicity that seemed to slice into him. "It was your only goal, I assume. That and extracting private sentiments from me that you could sell to the tabloids."

"I never sold anything to the tabloids," he replied.

It was true. He'd given away those stories for free.

"I'm actually delighted to have the opportunity to discuss this with you," she said, with a strange light in her eyes, propping her elbows on the table between them. "I used to dream about doing this, though when I did, it was less *discussing* and more...beating at the side of your head with a stick of some kind. But, you know. Bygones."

"I'm afraid I'm not following you." He eyed her, and that light in her gaze. "Surely you are not complaining that I was *mean* to you? I know you were a sensitive girl back then, Molly. But really. There is a vast difference between *meanness* and a person simply not catering to you in the way you would like."

"Sensitive," she repeated, as if tasting the word and not finding she liked it overmuch. "Isn't it funny how that word is used as an insult? Think about what it means. Yes, I was very *sensitive* to your manipulations. And your father's. And—"

"Are you comparing me to my father?" His tone was light, but he doubted his gaze matched. "Do you dare?"

If he expected Molly to back down, he was in for a disappointment. She only gazed back at him, her expression neutral enough, save the arch of her brows.

"My mistake," she said in a cool tone designed, he knew, to rub him the wrong way. It worked. He hated that it worked. "There are no similarities. Your father isolated a woman here, constantly veering back and forth between treating her as a lover or treating her like the help. Either way, she was an object entirely at his whim. There is, naturally, no overlap whatsoever between the two scenarios."

"Is this an example of the sensitivity you claimed not to have?" he asked darkly.

"Am I the sensitive one, Constantine? It seems you're the one having a reaction."

He was having any number of reactions, and he doubted very much that she would like it if he shared them with her. He did not care how long it took him to get himself back under control, so long as he managed it. He did not like how close he'd come to losing control altogether. He did not care, at all, for how this woman affected him.

But he didn't walk away from her or this situation he'd created, either.

"I believe you were going to tell me how it was that I hurt your precious teenage feelings, making me somehow responsible for your lack of self-confidence at the time." His shrug, it turned out, was no less a weapon than hers. "Though I think you will find that many a teenage girl is in the same predicament. It is the *teenage girl* that does it, not me."

"How many teenage girls do you know who had their confidences funneled directly to the gossip rags?"

He eyed her. "Do you imagine that I will apologize for this?"

Her lips curved, but there was only frigid cold in her gaze. "A Skalas? Apologize? The very earth would tremble."

"If you resent finding yourself in these crosshairs, Molly, I would suggest that you address yourself to your mother. As she is the one who put you there."

Molly scowled at him. "I get it, Constantine. You didn't want a stepmother. Boo-hoo. It may shock you to discover that I didn't particularly want a stepfather, either. Particularly not one like your father, who was, at best, sadistic. And that's about the nicest thing I can think to say about him."

He made a scoffing sound, but she didn't subside. Instead, she leaned over the table, still aiming that scowl right at him. "It amazes me that you seem to think my mother, a housekeeper with no formal education whatsoever, managed the astonishing feat of *trapping* Demetrius Skalas, who was at that time the richest man on earth. *Trapping him.* What a joke. If she had that kind of power, why would she have stopped with a simple trap? Why wouldn't she have used her power to either make him a better husband, or, failing that, kill him off so she could live out her days as a very wealthy Skalas widow?"

Constantine couldn't say he liked either one of those questions very much. "You are naive in the extreme if you don't know precisely how your mother ensnared my father."

"Because… What? Demetrius Skalas, once again the richest man in the world—and also well renowned for the parade of women on his arm all throughout his marriage—suddenly tripped over one particular woman and could no longer function? My mother worked some kind of spell, is that it? And he was susceptible for only as long as it took to race off and marry her. Then, in another bit of magic, he became completely impervious to her in every way." She rolled her eyes. "Come on, Constantine. You can't really believe any of that."

He found his ribs were too tight, suddenly. He was too aware of his pulse, and the way it racketed around inside him. He glared at her, wishing the lantern light didn't make her look even more beautiful than she already was. Because the beauty was distracting, and somehow made the charges she was levying against his father—and against him—seem that much starker.

And something he almost wanted to call painful.

"Nothing you can possibly say to me is going to make me change my opinion of your mother, Molly," he said.

When he could speak with the voice that was only dark with warning, not bright with his temper.

"Of course not," she said quietly, her arctic blue gaze pinning him where he sat. "Because if you did that, you would have so many other unfortunate questions to ask yourself, wouldn't you? If you're wrong about my mother, then all the years you spent sandbagging her every move would seem…vicious, wouldn't they? If you're wrong about my mother, this price you intend to extract from me by naked days and romantic nights really does make you a monster, doesn't it? And that's not even getting into what you did to a lost teenage girl who could have used a friend. The less said about that the better, I think you'll agree."

"I think that's enough," he managed to growl.

"I'm sure it is," Molly said with a rueful little laugh that set his teeth on edge. "It gets scary straying that close to the truth, doesn't it?"

He was on his feet, though he didn't recall when he'd decided to move. Constantine stood over the table, staring down at her, and for all her talk of what was and was not a spell, he felt cursed.

She had haunted him for years. And over the past ten days, that haunting had only grown worse. Because everything had gone according to plan here, except his reaction.

He had wanted her to be lulled into a false sense of security. He had wanted her to stop worrying he might pounce on her at any turn and to embrace both the insistence upon nakedness as well as the sunscreen he ritualistically applied to her body every morning.

But while she seemed to have acclimated with ease, all Constantine seemed to do was lose sleep.

"You seem to have forgotten your place," he managed to get out.

But Molly rose, too, like a shimmering blue flame. She was a gloriously tall woman, no doubt used to looking men in the eye. Or looking down at them. Yet she had to tilt her chin to manage it with him, and Constantine found he liked that he did not loom over her as he normally did over women.

Because it put her mouth that much closer to his.

"You'd better teach me my place then," she shot back at him. "Don't you know? We Payne women have a terrible habit of casting spells on unwary men like witches of yore, then making them do our bidding. Behold my success, for it has made me…your plaything."

"Shut up," he growled at her.

And then he took her mouth in a fury.

It had been too long since that last kiss. It had been *too long*.

He found his hands on the sides of her jaw, holding her mouth right where he needed it. He kissed her and he kissed her, a wild taking. A claiming, possessive and dark.

He kissed her until he realized that if he didn't stop, he would take her right there, out on the terrace beneath the stars.

And that was not the plan.

Just as the fire that coursed through him was not the plan, because it threatened to undo everything. It got in his head, it made him far too hard, it made his hands move over her as if all he'd been put on this earth to do was worship the glory she wore so easily.

He kissed her until he thought it might break him, and then he thrust her away from him.

And took some solace in the fact that however wrecked he might feel, she looked worse. Her blue eyes had gone dark, needy.

The sound she made was of loss.

"Tonight is our last night here," he told her. "We have a series of extremely high-profile events to attend, Molly. Remember. This affair will be very, very public."

"Is it an affair? Or an impromptu bit of theater you've set up for your entertainment?"

But she didn't ask that quite as sharply as she might have. And he could hear the tremor in her voice. He could see the flush on her face and against the fabric of that dress of hers, the telltale press of her hard nipples, giving her away.

"Don't you worry about when our affair will begin in truth," Constantine said, dark and hot. "You'll know. You'll find yourself on your knees, begging as beautifully as you do anything else."

And then he left her there, still obviously trying to hide the fact that she was shaken before she could tell that he was, too.

CHAPTER SEVEN

MOLLY SHOULD HAVE EXPECTED, Constantine being Constantine, that the publicity tour he had apparently put together in his spare time—all while seeming to do nothing but drive her to the brink of distraction with his daily sunscreen ritual, then taunt her every evening—was comprehensive. And would catapult them to the forefront of every gossip's mind, not to mention every tabloid's main page, with a vengeance.

Because vengeance was his goal, and she needed to remember that. She had almost started to think that his goal was to keep her completely off balance, because he was succeeding at that, and brilliantly.

Though she thought she would rather fling herself from one of the Skiathos cliffs, like the Gothic heroine she told herself she was, than admit it.

That next morning he drove them both in a simmering silence to the Skiathos airport. His jet waited for them there, prepared to whisk them off across the world to Los Angeles, stop one on their world tour. It might look like a romantic interlude to some. It was meant to look like a happy accident of press appearances while engaged in some of that high-profile celebrity charity that famous and infamous people alike used the way teenagers used the hallways in their schools, all see and be seen.

But Molly knew the point of it was neither romance nor charity. It was her eventual humiliation. He'd said so.

"If we are attending some kind of gala event," Molly remarked as they started their descent into a surprisingly clear day over the Los Angeles basin, "does that mean that you have also selected my wardrobe? Or is this more naked time. That *will* cause a stir."

Across from her, Constantine barely looked up from the laptop that had consumed his attention for the whole of their flight. Too busy checking for mention of himself in several languages, she could only assume. Because it was too strange to think of Constantine Skalas actually *working*. Surely that was what Balthazar was for.

She couldn't have said what Constantine was for, save her own, personal destruction.

"Your role is simple," he said now. "Keep your mouth closed and act adoring. Easy enough, no?"

"Easy, yes," she agreed. "But unusual, cer-

tainly. I'm not exactly known as the shy and re-
tiring type."

Constantine slapped his laptop closed as the
jet's wheels touched the ground. His gaze seemed
to touch hers with a similar impact. "But you are
besotted, *hetaira*. You hardly know yourself. Your
body betrays you with the things it wants and you
tell yourself you ought to be horrified, when in
truth, all you are is wildly, madly in love. So much
so that it is astoundingly visible to all and sundry
and possibly even from space." Then his mouth
curved in that mocking way that always seemed to
pierce straight through her. She assumed he must
know that. "Or is that too much of a stretch?"

"Don't you worry," Molly said, as if trying to
soothe him. She smiled. "I'm very, very good at
my job."

But she was just as happy when his attention
was redirected to his mobile, because that had all
been…a little too close to the truth for her liking.

Because she had the terrible fear that despite
all her tough talk, she was more in danger when it
came to Constantine Skalas than she ever had been,
even back when they'd lived together in Skiathos
the first time.

Because the teen girl she'd been then had never
imagined he would look twice at her. Not really.
Whereas the grown-up version of Molly was a

little too aware that at any moment, there was the possibility he might kiss her again.

Or more.

Why hadn't he done more?

She had spent ten days wandering around naked all over his estate in Skiathos, pretending she didn't feel half-feverish at the thought, waiting for him to put his hands on her at any moment. To her dismay, it was nearly all she thought about, unable to understand why it was that he simply kept her…wanting.

Maybe the wanting was why.

If so, it worked. It drove her mad. She had lounged about near the pool every day, near the sun if not quite in it, imagining that every stray breeze was his touch. And even though ten days of forced idleness should have driven her crazy, she had never felt particularly idle. Too busy was she…imagining.

Because the things that had happened inside of her the first time he'd put that sunscreen on haunted her. Not to mention the things she'd done. God, the things she'd *done*… She still daydreamed about it. Those hands of his, all over her breasts. That hard thigh thrust between her legs. Her absolutely shameless display as she'd rocked herself against him… How she'd moved her hips, making no secret of the fact that she was pressing the molten, aching core of her femininity against his hard-packed muscles.

Deliberately. Desperately.

Molly wasn't sure why she hadn't died from embarrassment. Instead, she had lived. And now relived those moments, over and over and over again, and if she was honest with herself, not because she was attempting to browbeat herself with guilt and shame. Not at all.

She had managed to keep herself contained every other time he ran those hands, slicked with lotion, all over her skin. She had simply packed those sensations away as she did every time she stepped in front of a photographer. She felt as she was told to feel. She moved as she was told to move. She was a canvas who existed for others to paint their vision all over her.

It was harder than it sounded, but during the day, it worked well enough. Even at their typically fraught dinners, she did her best to funnel her feelings away while she dressed in what he'd left for her. And because she was dressed for his pleasure, she took the evening meal as an opportunity to vent her spleen.

The truth was, she'd gotten used to it. She had gotten used to Skiathos, and while the fact she had no choice but to be there again could never make her love it, she found herself becoming something like affectionate for the place, after all.

But it was when she went to bed in that bedroom that had been hers once before that everything she kept at bay all day long swamped her.

At first she thought it was just as well. He might excite her to a fever pitch, but there was nothing to say she couldn't handle her own pleasure as she pleased once she was alone.

Except she didn't.

Because Constantine had told her not to. It was as simple as that. And her own obedience to this man who made no secret of the fact that his aim was to destroy her appalled her. It made her wonder, not what spells her mother might have worked back in the day, but why she, personally, was cursed with an inability to treat Constantine as he deserved in turn. Or even think of him as she ought to.

But however appalled she might have been, she didn't disobey him.

And as they rode in the back of a limo through Los Angeles, a city she knew well, she had to assume that all of this was part of his game. Her uncertainty. Her feeling of being forever off balance. Even his rules about sunscreen and the clothes he insisted she wear, so that at all times, whatever touched her body was his. It was a game, all right.

What Molly didn't understand was why she kept playing right into it.

The house he took her to sat propped up high

in the Santa Monica Mountains that ran through the center of California's largest, most sprawling city. They took one of the canyon roads up from the valley floor, a winding, slow affair. Slowly they climbed into the foothills, one tight curve after the next, passing houses that defied gravity and nature as they clung to the sides of cliffs. A grand, if vertical, mansion next to what looked like an old cottage, all tucked away in that southern California lushness that always surprised her. Think of Los Angeles and what came to mind was traffic, but the city was much more than that. The mysterious hills, where coyotes roamed and some nights, it could seem as if civilization was far, far away. The famous beaches and beyond them, surprising pockets of charming little places that still felt small and close-knit. Old flower-children's retreats in far-off canyons, beautiful architecture, and the smell of citrus and salt on a sweet spring breeze. As she looked out her window now she saw hummingbirds darting between one blossom and the next, all of them bright and plush, and around them, great swathes of green and fruit-bearing trees. Outside, the air was scented with a hint of smoke, rosemary and sage, and the sweetness of too many flowers to name.

They made it to the top of the hill and stopped at its crest. The house they'd arrived at looked wholly unremarkable from the winding street outside. It

was overgrown with exuberant vines of bougainvillea that reminded her of Greece, thick curtains
of jasmine she knew would bloom at night, and an
invitingly green arched trellis that led to the unas-
suming front door of what appeared to be a very
modest bungalow.

Molly knew it wasn't. Even before she exited
the limo she knew that despite appearances, there
would be nothing modest about any place Constantine Skalas frequented.

And sure enough, the house cascaded down the
side of the cliff, a jumble of sleek modern levels
flowing in and out of each other, creating a poetry
of indoor and outdoor space. Rooms that were en-
closed had as few opaque walls as possible and the
rest was all glass, looking out over the enduring
tangle of the City of Angels, stretched out as far as
the eye could see. And because the day was clear,
she could actually see the thick blue ribbon of the
sea in the distance.

It was stunning. Because it was his. How could
it be anything else?

"We leave for the red carpet in two hours," Constantine informed her. And shook his head as she
began to speak. "I don't want to hear excuses about
how much time you need to make your appearance. You claimed you could appear in a garbage
bag, did you not?"

"I was being facetious."

He smiled, nothing but challenge in his gaze. "I want to see magic."

"Garbage bag magic?" She kept her voice light. "Who knew such a thing existed?"

But the intensity of Constantine's stare did not waver. "Magic, Molly."

"Then magic it will be," she assured him. What else could she say?

"My staff will assist you." He nodded toward a woman who waited there at the edge of the glass room, her gaze lowered.

Molly smiled at him. "You are too good, Constantine. Really."

And her reward was a searing, almost painful blast from those coffee-dark eyes.

A warning she really should heed, she knew. But she couldn't seem to do that.

Molly followed the woman down a series of exposed staircases, moving in and out of the glass enclosures. Then she led the way into a room that had been transformed into the kind of salon Molly knew best. Racks of clothing stood ready, and more, she saw a fleet of men and women she instantly recognized as stylists and beauty estheticians, armed with the tools of their trade.

Very well then. This was a test he wanted her to pass, and Molly did not *pass* tests. She aced them.

"What is this red carpet for, exactly?" she asked the woman beside her as she scanned the clothes provided. She recognized most of the designers from the cut of their garments, as clear to her as if they'd been labeled.

"It's a gala event," the woman told her, and then outlined exactly what charity the gala supported and more importantly, the expected celebrity content of its guest list as well as the kind of press expected.

"We do have some suggestions," the woman began.

Molly smiled at her. "I think I've got it. But thank you."

She remembered being interviewed by a journalist once who had spent the better part of the interview making snide, not particularly *passive* aggressive remarks about how low-maintenance and carefree she, the journalist, was. *She* couldn't imagine spending *twenty whole minutes* on her appearance, much less the hours and hours that Molly did. And she certainly didn't waste so much brainpower *worrying* about *clothes*.

Though, of course, she'd been speaking to Magda.

That is why, Magda had told her imperiously, *it is the words you type with your unmanicured fingers that go into magazines. While it is my face that graces the cover.*

There were a lot of things Molly found herself uncertain about lately, but fashion, style, and how best to use both as her best weapons were not among them.

She changed swiftly into the smock waiting for her, and then handed herself over into the clutches of the beauticians, making her preferences known when it came to nail polish, toenail polish, brow shape, and the cosmetics themselves. She and a makeup artist had a robust discussion about lip shade and a smoky or un-smoky eye. And when she told the hairstylist her concept for hair, he agreed, his eyes lighting up.

And then all of them got to work.

One hour and fifty minutes later, she stood before the mirror with her hastily assembled team around her. She took a look at herself from each side, critically. Then she lifted her gaze so she could see everybody standing behind her. And beamed.

"You are all absolute stars," she said, and meant it. "This is complete perfection."

Then she walked upstairs to present herself for Constantine's inspection, two hours to the second after she'd left his side.

And had the distinct pleasure of watching him do a double take.

He had been waiting for her with a drink in one hand, looking out one of the enormous windows over the city that lay before him as if displayed on a platter. He glanced at her, then looked back outside—only to whip that gaze back to her again.

She strode toward him, letting him take in the look she'd selected. "Does this garbage bag meet with your approval?"

For his part, Constantine was dressed in what should have been sober black tie, unremarkable in any way. But it was Constantine wearing it, so he looked not only faintly rumpled but as if the effort of standing upright was almost too much for him, so profoundly was he a creature who ought to have been horizontal. Stretched out lazily in the nearest bed, and not alone.

"I expected something ornate," he said, but she didn't think it was criticism.

Molly turned in a full, slow circle for him before he asked—or twirled that finger of his—so he could see the full effect. "You asked for starry-eyed adoration. And I think we can agree that I've delivered it."

She already knew how the pictures would look. She had picked the simplest gown on offer, in a deep, luxurious blue. It looked like nothing much on a hanger, but she knew the designer well and had known at a glance that it would hug her perfectly and more, make her skin look luminous. She had the makeup artist make her look fresh and dewy, with a little bit of glamour around the eyes, on the off chance she couldn't quite pull off full-on adoration at all times. And to top it off, the hairstylist had created a breathtaking bit of pony-tail art that made her look like the girl next door.

Molly looked like innocence personified, and next to Constantine, she might as well have taken out a billboard announcing that she was Little Red Riding Hood, and he the Big Bad Wolf.

She could see by the way he grinned, slow and sure, that he agreed.

"The only question," he said as he drew close, then took her arm in a possessive grip that made her whole body tighten, then melt, "is whether or not anyone will believe that a woman such as Magda could ever be innocent."

"Love makes innocents of us all," Molly said quietly, wishing those words sounded as arch as they had in her head. "Isn't that the story you're selling here? Magda, a known whore who is also the daughter of whores, is rendered into a Disney heroine at one touch of your wicked hand. What tabloid could resist such a lovely tale?"

He was still holding her arm, that hard palm of his wrapped around her bicep, which meant he was much too close. She knew his scent, now. She knew his heat. And the danger of his heavy-lidded gaze that only seemed to grow worse with time.

Or perhaps it was that she grew more suscep-tible with each day that passed.

"Why would anyone resist?" he asked, his voice rough.

And for a moment, while he gazed at her, she forgot where she was. She forgot who she was. The California sun streamed all over them both, but all she saw was the rich dark of his gaze. Her heart thudded. Her blood seemed to sing in her own veins, loud and clear.

When he turned away, steering her toward the door, she realized she had been holding her breath. And more, that she'd wanted absolutely nothing in that moment but to feel his mouth on hers again.

But Constantine did not kiss her that night. He waited.

First there was the red carpet in Los Angeles. Then it was a jaunt across the Pacific to Singapore, then on to Dubai, and then, in quick succession, Rome, Madrid, and then finally to Paris.

They had made exactly the splash Constantine had wanted. The world was obsessed with them. No one had ever seen Magda look so sweet, so smitten. No one had ever seen Constantine look even remotely possessive—of anything.

The public was hooked.

What worried Molly was her dawning realization that she was, too.

She was careful to remind herself—she tried to remind herself—that if he expected her to put on an act, he was likely doing the same. No matter how it felt sometimes.

In all, the trip took two weeks. It was a jumble of time zones, flashbulbs, and the flights in between, tucked up in that jet of his. Kept stocked, after the first week, with tabloids from too many countries to count. All featuring their faces.

"It makes a difference to actually *try* to make it on the cover of the tabloids, I suppose," Molly had said somewhere in the beginning of their second week. "A bit inside out, if you ask me."

"I want to be certain that for the rest of your career, no matter what happens, you will be asked about me," Constantine had told her, with that smile of his that let her know this was a part of his revenge he loved the most. He liked to study her over the edge of his laptop, where he did who knew what. "Of course, a girl can only model for so long. As you might imagine."

Molly had not shared with him that no one knew the expiration date on a model's career more intimately than the model in question.

"Handy, isn't it, that you can go right on being a bastard forever," she replied instead, smiling wide.

And had pretended not to notice it when she'd gotten a real laugh out of him for her trouble.

Because all the while, the tension between them grew. A tension she tried to tell herself had to do with his great revenge and only that revenge…

but she knew it didn't. It was rooted in the way he touched her. Every time skin met skin, an electricity that only seemed to rage brighter and longer between them flared. And never dimmed. It was every event where they were stood next to each other, always touching, always gazing adoringly at each other.

Always acting, she told herself.

Only acting, surely—though more and more, she feared that wasn't what she was doing at all.

They landed in Paris in the early afternoon and because it was Paris, Molly took extra time preparing herself for the evening ahead. That night, she went for more drama overall, but compensated for that with an understated face and a flat shoe that would be seen as edgy. Particularly amongst the fashionistas of France.

It was a typical evening. Too many pictures taken. Too many faces, all of them avid and insinuating, not much more than a big blur before her. Another formal dinner where she ate heartily no matter if she liked what she was served or not. Because Molly distinctly disliked the fact that as a model—a woman whose job it was to maintain a certain body shape—she was constantly observed when food was around. It tired her.

We must take our rebellions where we can, she told herself as she smiled at a sharp-eyed society doyenne seated near her, then ate a huge forkful of creamy pasta just to watch the other woman recoil.

Like many of these events on their little tour, there was also dancing. And no matter how many times she told herself that she was used to it, she wasn't. No matter how many times Constantine gathered her into his arms and looked down at her as if nothing else existed save the two of them, she wasn't ready.

You will never be ready, a voice inside her pronounced.

And in another sense, she'd been ready since she was sixteen.

Maybe that was why, when they made it back to a Parisian penthouse apartment that, like all of the Skalas properties she'd sampled on this trip, commanded astonishing views, Molly…lost it.

If this night went the way all the other nights went, she and Constantine would sit about drawing blood and scoring points over drinks. Then he would take himself off and she would find herself lying wide awake in another strange bed, her hands between her legs yet unable to give herself the relief she craved.

Tonight, she thought that going through this same routine of hers might kill her.

"I was promised a very specific kind of torture," she said, standing in the great living area with the City of Light shining in all around. Molly could hear that her own voice sounded…distinctly unhinged. "You made it perfectly clear this was supposed to be a real affair, or else how could you possibly destroy me at the end of it?"

Constantine, pouring the usual drinks at the bar across the room, turned. "I beg your pardon?"

"To be honest, Constantine, it seems to me that after all this jetting about the planet, not to mention starting off the whole thing with a one-way nudist colony, I deserve some kind of compensation."

"Why would you think that?" he asked mildly, though his gaze had gone glittery in that way that made everything inside her cartwheel about. She should have been used to it by now. And yet was not. At all. "Surely I cannot have given you any reason to assume that your feelings matter here? I did try to avoid it."

"Perish the thought," she said grandly. "I'm only looking out for your interests. If, after all, this is nothing but a little act we're putting on for the press, well. That's a different scenario than the initial bold threats that were issued. With, I suppose, a dose of compulsory nakedness from time to time, just to keep everyone honest?"

Constantine swirled the liquid he held in a heavy tumbler in one hand. His eyelids, already so seemingly sleepy, seemed to droop even lower. It made his gaze seem all the brighter.

"Why, Molly. I am shocked. Are you asking me for sex?"

Was she? But she knew she was. "And if I am?"

She didn't know what she was doing. Or maybe that was a cop-out. Maybe she knew exactly what she was doing. Maybe what she'd said to him was true, after a fashion. She was putting out all this effort. She was already linked with him in the press and everywhere else. The whole world thought she was engaged in a torrid affair with *the* Constantine Skalas, which did not horrify her the way it should have. Oh no.

Molly knew, keenly, that the sixteen-year-old idiot girl who'd been so enamored of him would have loved to find herself in this situation. Had, in fact, wished and dreamed and hoped for precisely something like this to have come along back then.

What she couldn't seem to handle—because the longing for him had become a pulsing thing between her legs, on the insides of her wrists, at her temples, in her throat, *everywhere*—was not getting the opportunity to actually have that affair.

Because she'd spent her whole life not having affairs.

Not only with Constantine Skalas, but with anyone. The world kept turning and people were out there having life-altering sex, apparently. All while Molly just writhed about in photo shoots, selling sex to the camera yet having none herself.

If he was going to blow up her life anyway, she might as well enjoy the fire while she burned. Why not?

And since she had the distinct impression that they were going to end up in bed together anyway, once he finished playing his little revenge games, Molly could admit that she took a certain pleasure in moving things along her own schedule.

Because she had the feeling it might very well be the only thing she would control when it came Constantine. Ever.

"I thought I made it clear," he said, still regarding her in that way that made her want very much to squirm. If she was a person who squirmed. Until tonight, she never had been. "If you want me, you must beg. I do not mean pretty words, though I fear I do require them. I will have you on your knees, naked, begging for the privilege."

"You really do like a pageant, don't you?"

He gave a very Greek sort of shrug, more his chin than his shoulder. "The only people who do not care for a pageant, *hetaira*, are those who know one will never be thrown in their honor."

"Fair enough," she murmured.

And it was one thing to want sex at last. Right now. But another to do what he was asking. To debase herself—

But who was she kidding? She had already debased herself to the moon and back for this man, and more, had loved it more than she'd hated it. What was a little more where that came from?

Letting out a long sort of breath—a soft sound of surrender—Molly reached around to the side, where the zipper of the current dress she was wearing was cunningly concealed, and zipped it down. She let the gown fall, then pool around her feet, then she kicked it aside.

She let him look at her for a moment, stood there in nothing but heels and a push-up bra, and then she kicked her shoes aside and pulled off the bra at the same time. It was so easy to undress, she thought a little wildly, even though it took hours to get her looks put together so she could look effortless in public.

That is because fashion is always about sex, a beauty editor had once told her grandly.

Tonight Molly agreed.

Naked, she glided across the room until she stood before Constantine. And the longer she looked at him, the more her heart thundered inside her chest.

And the slicker, and hotter, she felt between her legs.

"Beg," he ordered her, though his voice sounded slightly hoarse. Rough like his hands would be against her skin. "And make it good, Molly. I've been waiting for it for a long, long time."

Molly took a deep breath. She wanted to smile but found she couldn't.

Instead, she did the only thing she could.

The thing she'd been wanting to do for longer than she cared to admit.

She sank down onto her knees before the devil himself, tipped her head back so he could see her face, and begged.

CHAPTER EIGHT

AT LAST.

Constantine had waited so long. All the plotting. All the planning. The angry seed of vengeance that had been planted so long ago when his father had brought home a new bride. The small, wiry green shoot of fury that had developed when dreamy Molly, unaccountably, had shot to prominence as Magda.

Those years when he'd seen her face everywhere. Like a taunt.

And the exquisite, almost unbearable weight of what had dragged on between them now for nearly a month.

All for this.

This.

He would not say that he was used to her nakedness by now, for who could ever grow used to the sight of such perfection? He would sooner be dead than *used to* her.

But it was a different thing altogether to see her on her knees before him, graceful and gorgeous, and her head tipped up to him. Showing him, in case he'd had the slightest shred of doubt, that she hungered for him as he had always dreamed.

As he had been so sure she would.

Those arctic blue eyes were filled with heat, and Constantine could feel the weight of her hunger, its sharp claws, deep in his sex.

He could not wait to get inside her at last.

But all he did was swirl his drink in his glass and regard her idly. As if he was on the verge of boredom, but was trying to be polite, and he had the pleasure of watching her expression change as he looked at her.

He wanted her off balance, even on her knees. Maybe especially on her knees.

"That is a very pretty picture you are presenting to me, Molly," he murmured. "But that is your stock in trade, is it not? Pretty pictures. Pretty images. None of them you. You don't even use your own name."

"Did I misunderstand the stage directions?" she asked, and for some reason, the warm undertone in her voice, that thread of laughter when surely she should have been more mindful of her own surrender, was nearly his undoing.

Why was it that he could not seem to remember that what was happening here was serious? It was revenge. It was not the place for laughter. He should not have *liked* her.

"This is the trouble with beautiful women," he told her, and it was harder to sound as disaffected and jaded as he usually did.

But then, that was nothing new. He had been acting unlike himself when it came to Molly for far longer than he cared to recall.

Once again he was struck by how at ease she was in her skin. It was powerful. It made her seem something like mystical, adding to the glory of all her elegance. She settled back on her heels now, her breasts jutting out and her blue eyes gleaming with more than simply that hunger, now.

God, the ways he wanted her.

Especially when she smiled at him, that clever little curve of her lips that made him feel almost… silly. "I can't wait to hear the thoughts of an inveterate bedpost-notcher when it comes to women," she said. "Such things are always so incisive and hard-hitting, aren't they? And not at all patriarchal. I'm surprised you haven't already written a book on the subject, given how many women's names you've likely forgotten in your time. In the last week, even."

"Here is the thing about beautiful women," Constantine said again, refusing to rise to her bait. And then, as he considered it, astounded that he had to caution himself against such a thing in the first place. "A beautiful woman assumes that the *fact* of her is sufficient. That she need not think or do or say anything further. She exists, therefore that is all that need be expected of her. Her mere appearance on any scene should do all the thinking, doing, or speaking necessary, and she therefore assumes it will."

Molly's head canted slightly to one side, and he could no longer see any of that humor in her gaze. He should have been thrilled.

He told himself he was *thrilled*.

"Beautiful women are born with a face that they did not choose," Molly said quietly. After a moment that stretched on too long for Constantine's comfort, and he was the one who was in control. He was not the one on his knees. "And they are taught, over time, that people will react to that face. That strangers and loved ones alike will treat that face in ways that have absolutely nothing to do with the person behind it. You learn quickly that it is far better to simply present yourself and see what the reaction will be first. It's safer."

Something seemed to crackle between them, a new and more dangerous heat.

"Molly." Constantine said her name as if he had never tasted it in his mouth before. As if he'd never tasted her, when the reality was, he had never been the same since he had. "Nothing here is safe. Not for you."

He expected her to quail at that. To shrink down, there where she knelt before him, or shrivel a bit. To show some hint that she was torn into a thousand pieces as he could feel he was. As he would rather rip off his own head before showing her he was.

But instead, this confounding woman—his once-upon-a-time stepsister and his current obsession—smiled.

A big, wide sort of smile that made him want to shout out his frustration loud enough to topple the Arc de Triomphe. And yet, at the same time, it made him want to taste that smile himself. And then the rest of her.

Now.

Why could he not compartmentalize this woman as he had every other thing in his life?

"No one expects an intricately plotted revenge plot to be *safe*, Constantine," she said in mock quelling tones, and he could hear too well the laughter in her voice again. It was its own heat. "That would completely defeat the purpose of all that plotting. All the demands for naked sunscreen application. And our current grand tour of the romance that wasn't."

"If this is still a joke to you," Constantine said, and it hurt him to say it so lazily, but he managed it, "you might as well get dressed and take yourself off to bed. I told you the only circumstances under which we will have sex, Molly. Mockery is not among them."

She sighed a little. "I didn't realize we had to be as solemn and serious as death. I have to tell you, every story I've ever heard about the irresistible charm of Europe's finest playboy—and I think you know there are a great many stories—was a lie."

"Not a lie," he found himself retorting, when he did not need to respond to her provocations. Surely that she wanted him to respond was reason enough to refrain. "But not for you."

"I do enjoy being special," Molly murmured, her eyes too bright on his. "It's because of an experience I had when I was but a girl, you see. I'll tell you the story. Once upon a time, I had an evil stepbrother straight out of central casting who tied himself in knots to make certain I knew that while *he* was marvelous in all ways, I was destined for nothing at all but a life of sodden beige porridge."

"You must be speaking about Balthazar," Constantine replied, sounding significantly less lazy than before. "As I have never trafficked much in either the color beige, nor, happily, porridge. Sodden or otherwise. I would rather eat paste."

"Constantine." She knelt up again, raising her hands before her in what looked like supplication, even though he could see that all that heat and all that humor in her gaze was still right there. "You may have to lead me through this, as I'm a little rusty. I believe I picked up your deeply subtle attempt to let me know that merely kneeling before you as a woman you consider beautiful is not enough. But I'm afraid my begging skills aren't my strong suit."

"You can start by taking this seriously," he growled down at her.

And again, found himself something like confounded when all she did was smile wider, her eyes sparkling as if he just recited a love poem.

"I take this very seriously, actually," she said. She paused, almost as if she was debating something, but then blew out a breath. "I've never done this before."

"Beg for it?" He should not have felt that as a particular triumph, and yet he did. "I would not know myself, but I'm told it can add a certain… intensity. If not for you, then for me."

"Not so much the begging part," she said softly. "*It*, Constantine. The deed itself. This will be my first time and I want to thank you, in advance, for making it so soft, special, and beautifully caring."

Despite himself, Constantine laughed.

Hard.

Because the very idea of Magda, whose many lovers pranced about the planet giving interviews about exactly what it was like to sample one of the most beautiful women in the world—interviews that had long driven him mad—claiming to be *untouched*?

It was preposterous. Hilarious.

And somehow, it reset something in him. It settled him. If she needed to play games to get through this thing between them, then who was he to deny her that opportunity?

Constantine had always liked a game or two. It only made things more fun.

"Yes, of course," he drawled, trying—if not too hard—to sound more serious then. "I should have known at a glance that you were a virgin. I'm honored indeed that you have chosen to hand over such a glorious prize to your enemy."

Her smile grew practically beatific. "Constantine. You're not my enemy. I'm afraid that's always been a one-way street. Left to my own devices—those being, you know, when no one is mounting a coordinated campaign to crush my mother, taking both her money and mine—I don't think about you at all."

He shook his head, as if in disappointment. "Liar."

Then, finally, at that single growled word, her smile faded.

And he watched, transfixed, as the heat took over.

It was possibly one of the most beautiful things he had ever beheld.

He could see it all then on that beautiful face of hers. Heat, growing by the moment. Need and longing, a match for his own. And that same wild, incoherent desire that stormed through him.

"That is a lie," she admitted. And when he only held her gaze, she swallowed. "And I'm not kneeling here, naked yet again, to lie."

"I would hope not."

Molly's blue eyes were nothing like cold any longer. No hint of ice.

He felt the heat there like a punch to the gut. And lower still.

"Please," she said then, in a very different voice. This time she sounded husky. Greedy, at last. "Please, Constantine. I want to stop playing games. I want… I…" She faltered, and it seemed so real to him that he almost believed… But no. She was nothing if not an ace game player. She wasn't famous by accident. "I want you inside me."

And Constantine had played this out inside his head a thousand times. More. He had intended this begging scene to go on forever. He had wanted abject pleading. Perhaps proof of overwhelming arousal while she was at it, but certainly Molly on her hands and knees. A bit of time prostrate at his feet, even.

But in all his planning for this moment, it had never occurred to him that he might want her this badly.

He had wanted her, clearly. But he'd spent years telling himself that his attraction to her was all a part of his revenge and why it would work so beautifully. Not…a wanting in its own right.

And Constantine had made himself wait so long. He'd made himself hold back, though such a thing was not in his nature. He had waited and waited—

The waiting ended then. With a crack so loud inside him he was shocked it didn't tear down this building they stood in, then topple Paris to the ground.

He was shocked he still stood.

But in the end, it was that simple.

One moment he was worried about his plan, the next he was done.

Constantine reached down, unable to control himself a moment longer, and hauled her to her feet. He got his hands in the thick mass of her blond hair, shaking it free of its pins, then slammed his mouth to hers.

And the taste of her burned in him as it always did, so intense and so hot he could not believe he was not scalded.

But it wasn't enough. Not tonight.

He gathered her against him, plundering her mouth, and he wanted more. More of her taste. More of that sleek, glorious body of hers pressed against him. He could feel the points of her nipples, a sweet agony against his chest.

It was too much.

Everything about her was too much.

Because with every taste of her, every little way she melted against him, it was as if she was somehow blazing straight through all those boundaries he had always kept strong and secure. As if she was the one melting him, from the inside out.

Constantine needed to get inside her. He needed to vanquish her, once and for all, and no other way had worked yet. Surely that would.

It was the waiting, he assured himself. He had never waited for another woman, not in any sense. It had created an unreasonable hunger—but it would be assuaged soon enough.

Now, in fact.

Once again, all the plans Constantine had toyed with over the years seemed to disappear, in so much ash and smoke.

He lifted her up into his arms, then carried her over to the nearest long, deep sofa, where he laid her out like an offering. To his deepest, wildest greed.

The longings he dared not admit, not even to himself.

Molly might be a martyr, but she was his. *His.* And he intended to lick up every last drop of this sacrifice laid out so temptingly before him.

He tore out of his own clothes, tossing them aside in his haste to finally get as naked as she'd been in front of him all this time. And he only slowed when he saw her eyes grow wide. He watched as she flushed, a rolling splash of color that moved from her cheeks to her neck, and then all over those sweet breasts.

Sure enough, her eyes were dilated. Her lips were slightly parted, as if she found him just as overwhelmingly tempting as he found her.

Good, something in him intoned, like a vow.

And say what she might about enemies, he knew full well that she hated him. He wanted her to hate him. But that meant he knew that if she was looking at him like this, she meant it.

That gave him a little sliver of space to breathe in.

Better yet, to remember who the hell he was.

To slow it down and take control, before he exploded like an untried boy.

It almost felt like a blessing when he stretched himself out over her, there on that long couch. They both fit, if closely, and he could prop himself up on one elbow. Then look down at the work of art before him.

He took his time looking.

"Constantine..." she began, and there was a little break as she said his name.

He was already hard enough to hurt. But that catch in her voice really took him over the edge.

"Quiet, *hetaira*," he ordered her, dark and low. "This is not a time for talking."

Then he leaned down and set his mouth to her breast. He toyed with her hard nipple with his tongue while his hand busied itself with its twin.

Molly arched up against him and cried out, and so he kept going. Back and forth between each of her lovely, perfect breasts as she writhed and bucked and then, to his delight, shuddered into her first release since long, long ago in Skiathos.

She was so responsive it made his chest feel tight.

She was so responsive he *ached* to thrust himself deep within her, now.

But he didn't. Not *right now*, anyway.

He took her mouth again and settled himself over her, aware on some level that he was rushing things. That he had wanted, badly, to lay her out like a feast and take his time with each and every course.

But he couldn't seem to do it. He couldn't seem to wait another moment.

He fished around for his trousers, pulling out protection and sheathing himself with one hand. Molly's arms moved around his back to hold him, and Constantine had never been aware before of how good it felt to have a woman grip him like that. While her eyes were so wide, her face was still flushed, and she was already looking at him as if he performed miracles.

Just wait, he thought with dark pleasure.

But the waiting, at last, was over.

He settled the broad head of his sex at her entrance, reveling in her softness. Her sweet molten heat.

Below him, Molly pulled her lip between her teeth and nearly undid him with that alone, then gazed at him as if she was close to overwhelmed already.

When they hadn't even started.

"Hold on," Constantine advised her.

And then, finally, he began to thrust deep inside her—

Except he didn't.

Because he felt what could only be the innocence he had thought was a fine joke she'd made. A game she wanted to play.

But it was no joke.

Molly Payne—*Magda*, for all that was holy— lay beneath him, wincing slightly. Her nails were digging into his back, she was holding herself taut, and she was a virgin.

A virgin.

Constantine knew that this could not be. It could not.

Because if she was a virgin, that meant that he

did not know her at all. And more, that every single thing he had thought about her as he'd plotted out his revenge was wrong. That he'd been completely and utterly off course.

And if he was wrong about something he had long since accepted as an incontrovertible fact, what else was he wrong about?

Something in him pitched, then rolled.

"Molly…" he gritted out, in genuine pain.

But she scowled at him, this impossible woman. This *virgin* in the body of a *hetaira*, the ancient Greek term for a courtesan.

How could he have been so wrong about her?

"Don't you dare, Constantine," she gritted out at him, her scowl deepening. "Don't you dare stop now."

And then, to his astonishment, she thumped him one in the ribs.

Hard.

CHAPTER NINE

IT HURT, BUT MOLLY had expected it would.

She'd been told a thousand stories of terrible, horrible pain the first time, but people didn't seem to let that stop them from having sex. She didn't intend to let it stop her.

Because there was something right on the other side of the pain. Something almost seductive, like a new kind of fire. Molly knew that no matter what, she wanted to taste it.

For his part, Constantine looked poleaxed. He stared down at her, an expression she couldn't begin to interpret on that beautiful face of his.

And to her impatient fury, he didn't move.

So she did.

Molly might not have done this before, but she understood the mechanics. Or she understood them well enough, anyway, to lift her hips and try to press herself into that bright, sharp pain. Especially when it made him tight all around her, that astonishing body of his nearly vibrating as he held himself still.

"Molly—"

But she ignored him, rocking herself against that insistent press of his need until it hurt too much to bear. Then she pulled in a ragged breath and impaled herself.

And then lay there beneath him, panting.

Impaled and panting.

"That was very foolish," Constantine gritted out, in dampening tones.

"Only if it's bad." Molly laughed a bit at that, aware that it was shaky at best, but that didn't make her stop. "Is it going to be bad?"

And he still didn't look…quite like him. Something of that internal storm that so marked him was gone. Or not gone, exactly, but not the same. His dark gaze seemed flooded with gold.

Meaning she did, too.

He shifted over her so he could brush moisture she hadn't known was beneath her eyes away with his thumbs, as he held her head in place. Not in a way that made her feel held down, but in a way that made her feel precious.

She melted a little at that, inside and out.

"No," he said gruffly, his gaze intense. "I can promise you, it will not be bad."

And then he kissed her.

Molly found it was different from the kisses

that had come before. She would have said it was sweeter, but this was Constantine—and he was *inside her*. What sweetness could there possibly be?

And yet she thought of the honeyed sweetness she'd eaten in Skiathos, the richness on her tongue.

Constantine was better.

He kissed her and he kissed her, as if he wasn't buried deep inside her body. As if there was no hurry whatsoever. His chest brushed against her breasts as he held her face, and she hadn't thought that she was tense at all until she felt herself relax beneath him. Until she was melting into that kiss, pouring herself into the dance of his tongue and hers.

And slowly, surely, everything changed.

Until she felt as if both of them were liquid sunshine, tangled all around each other. The newness, the shock of his penetration began to change, too, rolling into a kind of molten thing. Bright. Warm, then hot.

Then hotter still, laced through with all that shine.

And only when she sighed a little against his mouth, running her own hands up and down the glorious planes and muscles of his back, did he lift his head and smile down at her.

She thought he was about to say something, likely something cutting and indisputably *him*.

But instead, he began to move.

And it was unlike anything she had ever experienced before in her life.

The heat of it. That unbearable, unimaginable slide, each one hotter than the last. Each one sending intensity and sensation searing through her. Into her limbs, lighting her up, making her dig her heels into the sofa they lay on so she could lift herself up to meet each impossibly beautiful thrust.

She'd spent her whole life posing for pictures and pretending, but this was real.

This was him, and her, and a slick joining that changed her every time he plunged deep inside. Changed her, then taught her.

Then it made her new.

Until she not only couldn't tell the difference between the two of them, she lost track of all those differences she'd maintained within herself, too.

This was too real for separations. This was too powerful.

Molly felt a different kind of quaking come over her and almost protested, because it was too soon. She wanted this to go on forever. And she couldn't tell if she cried because she knew it couldn't or because of the sudden surge of wildfire ecstasy that ripped through her, making her arch up against him and cry out.

She thought she might even have said his name.

But he didn't stop. He kept going, and that explosion shifted as his thrusts grew harder, more demanding.

All that golden light turned to fire. And her whole body seemed to light up, burning red and hot from the inside out.

And he knew. She could tell he knew, because he gathered her beneath him, his hands gripping her hips, as he pounded into her.

Molly met him, reveled in him, and to her surprise, shattered once more.

And that time, heard her name on his mouth as he followed.

She could feel a kind of oblivion beckoning, but she fought it off, because she didn't want to miss a moment of this. Of Constantine, his face next to hers and that remarkably powerful body of his laid out over her as if wanting her that much had made him weak.

How had she missed out on this for so long?

But on the heels of that thought came another one, and she almost made a sound in response. What if she had given in to one of the many invitations she'd received over the years and done that with anyone but Constantine?

She shuddered at the thought.

And nothing had been settled between them, but she didn't care. Because Molly might have been lost as a sixteen-year-old girl, but she'd been perfectly clear about one thing. That it was him. That it had always been and would always be him.

And she'd been right.

"Come," he said in a low voice.

Molly didn't have time to think about how or why his voice was different, only that it was. Because he was lifting her up, hoisting her into his arms as if she was one of those dainty, tiny girls who men were always toting about as easily as they heaved pints to and fro.

She felt a delicious sort of softness everywhere. She liked it. And so she did nothing at all but tuck her head beneath his chin, the better to contemplate the gorgeous strength of his collarbone, his neck, the underside of his jaw as he moved.

He carried her into the bedroom he'd claimed in this penthouse when they'd arrived, then brought her to a large, ornate bed that looked like the sort of thing whole French revolutions had been fought to protest.

Fitting, really, for Constantine Skalas.

He placed her down on the grandiose bed, then straightened, looking at her with a dark, unreadable look on his face that probably should have made Molly feel self-conscious.

But it didn't. Nothing could. Not when she felt like this, loose and beautiful and made entirely new.

His jaw tightened, and he turned, walking off into what she assumed was the en suite bathroom.

Sure enough, she heard the sound of water, and for once, was perfectly happy to simply stay where she was and wait to see what might happen.

Constantine was there at her side again in a moment, with a warm, damp cloth he pressed between her legs, and that was what made her suddenly feel...vulnerable.

"I had no idea that you were serious." His voice was almost too low to hear, a thread of darkness between them. Almost. "It never occurred to me that you could possibly be an innocent."

"Not anymore," she said brightly, and she didn't know what to do with that look in his eyes. She didn't know what to do, so she got back onto her knees, and ran her hands over his chest where he stood beside the bed. She reveled in the feel of her palms against his skin, his muscles, *him*.

"Molly."

Her name was a command, but she had no intention of heeding it. She let her hands wander where they would until one made its way down that fascinating arrow of hair to find his sex. Almost accidentally.

He was so hard, though not as hard as he had felt inside her. She wrapped her fingers around the width of him and he thickened, and Molly smiled. Because that, too, felt like a power she wished she'd known she'd had all this time.

"Molly," he said again, now sounding very nearly stern. "I do not think—"

"Can we do that again?" she asked, smiling up at him. She tipped herself forward so she could rub her aching nipples against his chest and taste all the parts of him she'd admired on the walk here. His corded neck, his bold jaw. "Please? I'm begging."

He made a low sound, but then his mouth was on hers again. And he was picking her up and turning her, rolling with her down onto that wide bed, until they were tangled up with each other again.

Constantine rolled to his back and let her explore him, but when she went to take his hardness in her mouth, he gripped her beneath her arms and hauled her up the length of his body.

"I want to," she said.

"We do not always get what we want, Molly," he told her, then kissed her until she melted against him once more.

He taught her how to sit astride him, then take him deep inside her from that different angle.

She rocked her hips against his, staring down at him in a kind of wonder. He looked up at her, his expression so fierce, his hands moving almost restlessly from her breasts to that place where they were joined.

He pressed a thumb down hard at her center

and she dissolved, almost sobbing out at the sharp pleasure of it.

Then he flipped her over onto her belly and came into her from behind. He slid one arm beneath her hips to lift them at an angle so that he could pound his way into her, once again taking her from the middle of one explosion and throwing her like a catapult straight on into another. And another still.

And when the last one hit, she heard him roar behind her.

Then she knew no more.

Molly didn't know what woke her, or how she knew that it was later. Much later, by her guess, and she knew instantly that Constantine wasn't in the bed with her. She'd slept but she'd been always aware of him beside her, wrapped around her, hot to the touch.

She sat up, her heart pounding at her as if in fright, but then she saw him.

He stood by the window, and for once, she got to gaze upon his glorious nakedness instead of the reverse. The lights of Paris flowed all over his perfect form, making him seem unreal. Like one of the statues in the Musée Rodin, where she had spent many a stolen afternoon while at loose ends in the city.

He put them all to shame.

"Constantine?" She hardly sounded like herself, but that didn't shock her. She didn't feel like herself either, not any longer.

She felt like his.

He didn't turn toward her, and yet she knew, somehow, that he had heard her all the same. A small, shivery thing teased the nape of her neck.

"I hated your mother long before I met her," Constantine said, his voice gravelly, his gaze on the city before him. "I hated the idea of her, probably before my father ever met her. But then, there she was. And she had a name and a face, and told me to call her Isabel, as if we were friends already."

Molly had spent her life wanting to have this conversation, and now that it was happening, she wanted no part of it. She wanted to fly across the room and throw her body against his, hoping that could distract him from whatever he was about to say. But just as he seemed to stand there, frozen solid at the window with Paris at his feet, she couldn't seem to move, either.

She could only watch the light move over his dark form. And wait.

He seemed to grow even more frozen as she watched. "But as luck would have it, my new friend Isabel gave me more than enough reason to hate her, personally." Constantine let out a laugh, though there was no humor in it. It sounded like a weapon, and this time, it wasn't one aimed at her. Why did that make her ache? "She *tried*, you see. She tried so hard. Not just to make my father happy, a doomed endeavor if ever there was one. But she went out of her way to try to love me, too."

He turned then, and Molly caught her breath. Because his face was a mask of anguish. Sheer torment. His eyes blazed with it, and she hated that, too.

"Constantine. I don't understand—"

"And how dare she love me so easily?" Constantine gritted out, as if she hadn't spoken. "When my mother's life was a spiral of despair. When my own mother had never been any good at loving anyone or anything because she was so focused on my father—anything to get his attention, good or bad. How dare a stepmother come along and try to do what she had never managed?"

That hit Molly like a blow. Hard into her belly.

She whispered his name. And he laughed again, that awful sound.

"Your mother was *kind*, Molly. Understanding. *Warm*. And oh, how I loathed her for it." He moved toward her then, and it felt like fate. Like doom. Then he stopped at the end of the bed and it felt a whole lot more like heartache. "But then you came."

"You don't have to do this," she managed to get out.

Maybe she meant, *Please don't do this*.

"But I do." He raked a hand through his hair as if he would rather have put it on her. She wished he would. And her heart was beating so hard against her ribs that she was surprised she wasn't rattling with the impact of each hit. "You were so soft. So astoundingly innocent."

"I think you mean stupid."

Constantine shook his head. "It was obvious to anyone who laid eyes on you that you could be easily chewed up and spit out and more, would never have the slightest idea what had happened to you."

It was a searing sort of pain, she found, to imagine her former self like that. Particularly as she knew it was true. And more, could see too well the gap between the girl she'd been then and the woman she'd become.

"Again, I think the word you're looking for is *stupid*," she managed to say. "All I knew of the world was the village I came from. Our neighbors might not have liked my mum much. They might have watched me a little too closely, forever on the hunt for evidence that I was either like Isabel or looked a bit too much like one of their sons, since Isabel never named my father. But at least I knew my place there."

"You had no business turning up in our world, Molly. You weren't made for it. You made the terrible mistake of imagining that people, at heart, were basically good. No doubt another gift from your mother."

"Yes," she said quietly. "You treated me like a friend and I believed you meant it. I've had a long time to beat myself up for that, Constantine. A lot of years to regret it, but do you know what? I don't. I would rather see the world as more good than bad. Or what would be the point of living in it?"

"How can you possibly continue to be this naive?" he asked, his voice filled with sadness and something like wonder at once. "The fashion industry should have succeeded where I failed and beaten this out of you years ago."

Her smile was rueful then. "Oh, it did. So did you, Constantine. But cynicism is a choice. And I decided I would not choose it, despite all provocation."

It hadn't always been easy, because there was a certain ragged pride to be taken in weathering the storms of a volatile industry. Not to mention fame, fortune, and the joys and horrors inherent in both.

But she had decided, with great deliberation, that she would rather be happy.

Wasn't that why she'd sought Constantine out? Oh, she'd told herself it was to face down the architect of her mother's financial ruin. She'd assured herself it had less to do with her own demons and far more to do with protecting Isabel.

Yet she knew better. Deep down, she had known

that she was never going to be happy until she either exorcised the devil…or embraced him.

He was staring at her as if she'd sprouted new heads. "The Skalas family has ever been a pit of snakes. I would rather have gone off to war than sit down to a family dinner when I was a child. You were woefully unprepared. Outgunned and outmaneuvered before your plane landed on Skiathos. I had every intention of snapping you like a twig. I wouldn't have thought about it twice. If anything, your total destruction would have amused me."

She cleared her throat. "My recollection is that you did precisely that. And happily."

Constantine let out a small, harsh sound. She could not call it a laugh.

"No, Molly. Not quite. Because you lit up when you talked about your mother."

Molly's voice hardly seemed to work any longer. "Is that a bad thing?"

His smile was merciless. "You knew her flaws, but you loved her. It was obvious. It made your whole face change even as you shared your frustrations with me. And the stories you told me, your little village secrets, did something I thought was impossible." That smile carved a deeper groove on his beautiful face and she understood, then, that his lack of mercy was aimed at himself for once. Not her. "You made me feel sympathy for Isabel, Molly. And I couldn't forgive it."

"Constantine…" she whispered.

"I never sold your stories to the tabloids, Molly. I was so determined to punish you for the things you made me feel that I gave them all away. For free."

Molly sucked in a breath at that. Her head was spinning. She had so many questions she wanted to ask him, but he was still glaring down at her in that stern, uncompromising way that should have made her faint.

Or something better than fainting, maybe. Something to address the way she prickled all over with that heat she now knew all too well.

"I don't require these confessions from you," she told him then. "I don't even want them."

She wanted to tell him she forgave him, but she didn't quite dare. Even if, as she let that notion take root in her, she knew it was true. Or she would never have taken off her clothes for him. She would certainly never have writhed about in his hands on that first day, all abandonment.

But there had been something about all those sun-drenched days on the island. Something about baring her skin and letting the breeze and the light find her wherever she was. Something about opening herself wide to Constantine's gaze and never wavering, never hiding, never falling apart.

Molly had forgiven him, yes. But she'd forgiven herself, too.

"I do not care if you want this confession," Constantine said tightly, as if this was a fight they were having. He certainly looked as if he was prepared to wade into battle, so tautly did he hold himself. "And despite all that, I'm sure I would have forgotten you in time. Isabel's relationship with my father didn't last, because nothing my father touched ever lasted, except the fortunes he hoarded. You were no threat. I could have gone quite happily about my life and never thought of you again, Molly. That was the goal all along."

She found herself staring back at him at that, mutely, not certain how to respond to that, much less the ferocity she could see stamped all over him.

"But instead, you became Magda. And you were everywhere. It began to feel not only as if you were hunting me, but as if you had played me from the start." His laugh then was dark. "There I was, the jaded and worldly Skalas son, stamping out an innocent for my amusement the same way my father had always trodden on anything that dared attract his notice. But no. That whole time I thought I was crushing you into the dirt, you had one of the most famous women in the world right there inside of you. Ready to come out the moment you left Skiathos and escaped my family. You became my obsession."

"I can't imagine why you would care what happened to me."

"Can you not?" His voice was a bitter lash. "Because I felt guilty, Molly. *Guilty.* You are the only thing I have ever felt guilty about in my life. Because for all I have always reveled in sin, for all I have sought out the darkness and the lowest of places, you did not deserve what I did to you. *And I knew it.*"

Now there was no stopping the way her heart catapulted against her chest. Now there was no hope of doing anything but sitting there, waiting to see what he would lob at her next. What mad grenade. What bomb she wouldn't see coming.

"Now it turns out that once again, you have shamed me," he said quietly. Ferociously. "Your innocence is my guilt made new. It proves that all along, I was never who I thought I was. And you… You have been even more pure, from the start, than I imagined anyone could be."

Molly felt turned inside out. Or maybe she only wished she had been, when all she could see was the rich darkness of his gaze turned bleak.

"This is a lot of talk of guilt and shame," she said. She found she could move then, so she did, crawling down the length of the bed until once more she could sit there before him, her knees beneath her. "And it seems to me that if we're going to spend the night castigating ourselves for the de-

spoiling of innocence, there should be more de-
spoiling. Don't you think?"

"You are not hearing me," Constantine thundered at her then. "You are the only thing on this
earth I have ever felt for, Molly. First it was guilt.
Then it was fury. And now—"

"Constantine," she said, desperate and greedy,
her heart a great clatter. Needy and sure, at last.
Absolutely sure what this was—what this had always been. "Shut up."

Then she launched herself at him.

And he caught her.

Molly might not have known what she was
doing, but she knew it felt good.

And this time was different all over again. This
time was slow. Constantine put his mouth on every
inch of her body, as if committing her to memory,
one lick of heat at a time.

He settled between her thighs and drank deep
from the heat of her core, until all she could do
was sob out his name like a prayer.

It felt that sacred.

Then he set her before him on her hands and
knees and took her that way, a slow, delirious
rhythm that made every part of her body seem to
come alive. Then burn bright.

Only when she was sobbing again—but this
time in the grip of that fiery need—did Constan-

tine flip her over, gather her beneath him, and drive them both home.

When she woke again, it was morning.

Daylight poured in through the windows, bright and sweet. Molly felt deliciously battered from head to toe, and as she stretched she laughed as she found so many interesting tugs in new places.

She did not see the note until she sat up and looked around for Constantine. He was nowhere to be found in the vast bedchamber, but the note had been clipped to the pillow beside her.

She picked it up, trying to make sense of the words written across the heavy card stock in a slashing, dark hand.

It was a simple message, direct and to the point.

Molly felt it like a stab wound through her heart.

YOUR DEBT IS PAID IN FULL.

CHAPTER TEN

CONSTANTINE FLEW BACK to his antiseptic penthouse in London, a modern masterpiece of low-slung furniture and strange objects that he found neither artistic nor functional. He hadn't chosen any of it himself. It was the work of the sort of interior design firm who catered to wealthy clients like the Skalas brothers, as it meant their work was always aspirational. The flat had been the subject of at least six different fawning articles about Constantine's *keen eye* and *flair for esthetics*.

It looked like a bloody surgery, he thought now.

But then, that was why he'd chosen it and let the firm run wild. He didn't want his home to be anything like the house in Skiathos. Memories lurking behind every door, rooms filled with art and nostalgia and ghosts. *Feelings* oozing from the walls. He had wanted his primary residence to stand as a visual representation of what he was.

Not the playboy, but the sharp-edged angel of vengeance he had made himself into.

He looked around the clean lines and soulless expanse of the penthouse and told himself he was fine. *Terrific*, even.

Constantine experimented with that theory upon his return to the Skalas & Sons London headquarters, dedicating himself to his work in a way he never had before. Meaning, visibly. He showed up at the office, did not send his usual proxy to board meetings, and generally turned the place on its ear by destroying the long-held fiction that he was the useless Skalas brother who did nothing at all, as a vocation.

And it was only after his trusted assistant suggested, very carefully, that he rethink his approach to the people who believed the hype about him—that he was lazy, sybaritic, more often to be found facedown in a sea of women than in the boardroom, and if he wished to change this that he do so at a more sedate pace—that Constantine accepted the fact that he was not, in fact, fine.

In any way.

If he was brutally honest with himself, he wasn't sure that he would ever be anything like fine again.

Because he had excavated entirely too many of his own deep, personal motivations, and the feeling that left in him was unbearable.

Constantine preferred the clarity of revenge. The

force and thrust of a life committed to nothing but vengeance. Every temper, every dark *feeling*, every wild and stormy thing within him—it had all been excused by his focus on getting even with Molly.

And through her, at last, Isabel.

Now all he could think about was Molly. That wasn't new. But the way he thought of her had changed. Instead of brooding over what he would do to her and the many ways he would crush her and her mother to dust, he woke in the night in a fever of need. Instead of finding ingenious new ways to put pressure on Isabel, he found himself lapsing into daydreams about sunny afternoons in Skiathos and the sheer glory that was Molly on her knees before him, smiling up at him as if she wanted him.

As desperately and comprehensively as he wanted her.

Constantine suspected he had changed. That Molly had changed him, somehow, with her frankness and her laughter and that spirit of hers that had seemed to bloom brighter the more she was tested. The more he had tested her, the stronger she had seemed.

His revenge had backfired spectacularly, loath as he was to admit it, even as one week turned into another, then another still, and he was as unsettled as he'd been when he'd left Molly in Paris.

Because everything was different. *He* was different, and he disliked it intensely.

It was possible he disliked *himself* intensely.

Because he'd seen himself too clearly. He could not seem to claw his way back from that.

"You do not sound well, brother," Balthazar commented when Constantine finally gave in and called him. He told himself it was only because his brother, too, knew the lure of revenge. And the particular way a woman could twist it all around—for how else was there to explain Balthazar's shockingly uncontentious marriage? "And how can that be? For I have never seen you look as happy as you did while engaged in your little experiment with flashbulbs and infamy."

"You're the last person in the world who should believe a press release," Constantine said tersely, glaring out at London as if his brother's face hovered there above the Shard.

"I would never believe a press release," Balthazar returned with a laugh. A *laugh*. Constantine still couldn't believe his older brother *laughed* these days, as if it was an ordinary, everyday thing instead of wholly out of character for the man he'd been until now. "But I'm referring to the expressions I saw on your face. Please remember, I actually know you. And more, am all too aware that you would make an absolutely dreadful actor."

"You're confirming my aptitude, then. For I assure you, it was all an act."

"If you say so." Balthazar was quiet for a moment, and Constantine could hear the sound of the sea in the background. It made him wish, with a deep passion he would have sworn could not possibly exist within him, to return to Skiathos.

To go back in time, and stay there for far longer than ten days, with nothing to do but appreciate Molly's sun-kissed limbs. And this time, not to *wait*.

His fist was clenched so tightly his bones ached. He forced his palm open, scowling as he did it.

"But why do you use the past tense?" Balthazar asked at last. "Do I dare even ask this question?"

"Molly has paid her debt to me in full," Constantine said. His voice sounded gritty. Rougher than it should have, and he was afraid he gave far too much away.

Surely this is why you rang your brother in the first place, a voice in him said testily.

Constantine rubbed his aching hand over his face, wishing he knew how to do more than *want*.

On his end, Balthazar made a considering sort of sound Constantine opted not to interpret. "Has she indeed. That is enterprising of her."

And Constantine had half a mind to throw his mobile across the cavernous great room he had heard described as *containing a loftlike vibe*.

Surely a little bit of destruction would liven the place up. Chip one of the sharp edges of his furniture that was decidedly not made for human habitation. This was a flat to admire from afar, or peer at in the pages of architectural magazines, not *live* in. Because Constantine did not *live* anywhere. He traveled between places and personas, always with the same goal in mind—revenge.

But now he had no goal and all his years of plotting vengeance sat heavily in him. He wanted to take the strange overly modern pieces in this flat and hurl them out one of his vast windows. Because it did not escape his attention that he had taken Molly on a tour of only his most beautiful properties. As if he had needed to make sure that a creature as beautiful as she was could only ever be surrounded by similar beauty.

As if he had imagined that he could bask in both. He had.

Now he stood in the reality of his life, such as it was, without her. Without the idea of her that had sustained him for years. And without the live, flesh-and-blood woman who had turned him inside out.

And it was cold. Impersonal. Incomprehensible in places.

He was all of those things.

And here he was on the phone to an older brother who had only ever been another soldier in the same dreadful foxhole. It had never occurred to Constantine that a brother could be—or should be—anything else.

But he wanted...

The mawkishness almost drove him to his knees, but he knew. What he wanted was a friend. Constantine certainly had none of those. If he wanted one, he would have to take his chances here.

And so, feeling very much as if he was flinging himself off his own balcony in lieu of his terrible, uncomfortable furniture, he told Balthazar... everything.

Everything he'd told Molly. And more besides.

When he was done, he felt sick. And something like hollow. And his head pounded so hard and erratically that he wasn't entirely sure he would hear Balthazar as he spoke.

Or maybe he only wished he wouldn't.

"A wise woman once told me that the best revenge of all is living well," Balthazar said. "And I must tell you, I've taken it to heart."

Constantine let out a dark laugh, not at all surprised to find that he was rubbing at his chest. As if he could press his heart back into place. "I live well enough as it is."

"The key is happiness, brother. If money could buy it, we would have had a far better childhood than we did."

"Happiness," Constantine said, pronouncing the word as if he wasn't sure how the syllables came together. Or if it might sting him while he worked it out.

"We could talk all day about the many sins of Demetrius Skalas," Balthazar continued. "And in fact, I would enjoy it. There's nothing about that man I admire and I take it as a personal challenge to make certain that I never hand on any part of him to my children."

"I will also take this challenge," said Constantine, who until that moment had never so much as considered the possibility that he would bring a child into this world.

And yet the moment he considered it, he could only think of one woman who could possibly be the mother to those children. His children.

Their children.

The thought of Molly, ripe with a child they'd made, made him hiss out a small breath as if he'd been punched deep in the gut.

"But we must also talk about our mother," Balthazar was saying, unaware that yet another sea change was sweeping his brother away as he spoke. "Both you and I went to such lengths to avenge her, though our approaches were different. I was furious about what had been done to her. You were furious at what was done to her memory."

"I fail to see the difference," he managed to say.

"You want her to be a saint, Constantine." Balthazar's voice was quiet, but direct. "When, like the rest of us, she was only a person."

"She is still a person," Constantine gritted out.

"You and I both know that isn't entirely true." His brother's voice stayed quiet. And powerful. "One of these days, when she has stopped clinging to what little life she has left in her, you and I will do what we must to honor her. But in the meantime, do you imagine that if she were not in that bed she would applaud what you were doing?"

"I like to think she would."

"Constantine. The only reason she stopped the downward spiral she was on was because she hit the bottom too hard to get up again. You know this. Our mother was a woman of grand obsessions. First with our father. Then it was her lover." And his voice was harsh then. For he had taken that lover down. "Then came many other lovers, and worse by far, the chemical inducements they provided her. But the one thing our mother was never obsessed with was her children. I choose to take that as a compliment. She couldn't take care of us. We could take care of ourselves, and we did."

Constantine stared out the window, but he didn't see London. All he saw was Molly. And then, almost superimposed over that face of hers that seemed to be lodged inside him, what dim memories he had of his mother before he'd lost her.

Because Balthazar was right. His mother had always been obsessed. Frantic and fragile. And while it was true that their father had been cruel to her—the way he was cruel to all who crossed his path—it was also true that she had never done much in the way of fighting back.

Not like Molly, who had found a way to stand tall in the worst possible circumstances. Even on her knees she had towered over him. Because that was the difference, wasn't it? A person either had that flame inside, or they didn't.

They either stood up or lay down.

He didn't think it was positive or negative, necessarily, but it did make him wonder why it was he was so determined to avenge a woman who would never, ever have avenged herself if given the opportunity.

And she would never have applauded you, that voice inside him told him harshly. *She barely noticed you as it was.*

He raked a hand through his hair. "When did you become a font of wisdom?" he asked his brother. Grumpily.

Balthazar laughed. Again. As if laughter was now a staple of his daily life. It was hard to imagine. Impossible, in fact, and yet he kept doing it.

"Right about the time you decided to call me for advice," he said then. "I suppose we can call this a brand-new day, Constantine."

When their call ended, Constantine did not fling his mobile across the room. He stayed where he was, staring out his windows until he saw London again. No superimposed faces. No ghosts. No regrets.

And when he did, he took a deep breath, then stalked out of his surgical flat and headed for one of his cars in the attached garage.

He drove out of the city, following a route he knew all too well. He took it as often as he could. At least once a month when he was in London, and he tried never to stay away for more than six weeks at a time.

Knowing full well that if their situations were reversed, his mother would not have maintained the same visitation schedule. In fact, it was likely she would never visit at all. It wasn't as if Constantine didn't know this. Of course he did.

But he couldn't say he'd truly *felt it* before now.

When he arrived at the long-term care facility where his mother waited, he took the steps two at a time, presenting himself to the duty nurse who knew him by sight.

"She's doing well," the cheerful woman told him as she ushered him down the same familiar hallway he'd walked for years, always lit up with that same, enduring thirst for vengeance that had animated his every action since he was twenty. "I do think it's that Good Samaritan of hers."

Constantine blinked at that. "I beg your pardon? A Good Samaritan?"

"Oh yes," the nurse said as they reached the door of his mother's room. She looked at Constantine with a slight frown between her brows. "She comes in most every week? I know I've mentioned her before. It's been years now?"

"Yes, of course," Constantine murmured, though he had no memory of any Good Samaritan. But then, would he have listened to anything that didn't serve that cold knife edge inside him? That intense focus on revenge? "How lovely."

Constantine supposed it was nice that someone else was visiting his mother. And yet when he walked inside and seated himself in the chair beside her bed, he knew it didn't matter. People made all sorts of claims about patients in the same state as his mother, and maybe they were right. But not about his mother. As he took her hand and looked down at her, at her still dark hair and soft face, he knew the truth. She was not trapped in there. On the contrary.

She was at peace.

A peace he knew she had never found while she was alive.

His conversation with his brother kicked at him. He looked into his mother's faintly lined face, looking far more at ease now in her endless sleep than she ever had when she'd been awake. She had forever been falling apart when they were children. As terribly as Demetrius had bullied his sons, he had bullied his wife even more. And when she did not cower or cry enough for his liking, he'd made sure to hurt her in other ways. Appearing with his mistresses in public. Making certain she always knew his unfaithfulness was epic and constant.

Constantine was not convinced he had ever seen her smile. Not a real smile. Not one that required anything more from her than good manners.

And he had loved his mother, truly he had, but looking back he could not say with any conviction that she had felt the same. They had been raised as much by nannies as by her, which had suited everyone.

Particularly when she had started taking lovers of her own.

And then, when Demetrius had thrown her out, it was not as if she had worked tirelessly to make sure she maintained contact with her children. She had always been far too busy recapturing what had been taken from her—or at least, that was his memory of the excuses she'd made at the time.

His father had delighted in calling her selfish, which had been laughable coming from him.

The truth was, Constantine thought now, she had earned that selfishness. She had earned any life she wanted after surviving Demetrius.

Why don't you deserve the same? something asked inside him.

But he put that aside, because he knew better. He was a Skalas male, not the victim of one. It was different.

"I'm so sorry, *mitéra*," he found himself saying, there alone in the room with only the quiet beeping machines that kept her alive for company. "I put you on a pedestal. And how was that so different from what my father did, if in reverse? Who knows how things could have been if I had only let you be who you were. Not what I wanted you to be instead."

He understood that the opportunity to know his mother had been taken from them both. And it was possible that had he come to know her, he might not have liked what he found. He understood that his mother was weak in many ways, but so, too, had his father exploited that weakness for his own amusement. Most of all, Constantine understood that he had been young when his parents had made the decisions that would mark them all.

Too young, and time had not been on his side.

Still…wasn't that what he did? He decided that there was a certain truth, and then he charged directly at that truth, forever. He would accept no complications, no complexities, no mitigating circumstances. Only what he accepted as truth existed, nothing else.

How else could he have missed the fact that Molly had been an innocent?

He thought that might haunt him forever.

Constantine kissed his mother on her soft cheek, whispered a goodbye he knew she couldn't hear, then rose.

And when he turned, there was a woman standing at the door.

For a moment he didn't recognize her. Perhaps he didn't want to recognize her.

He took in the pretty face, the quietly elegant way she held herself. And how startled her cool blue eyes looked as she beheld him.

Isabel.

The first thing he'd done after leaving Molly in Paris, when he'd returned to his offices in a fury, was to restore everything he had taken from Isabel over the years. And from Molly.

With interest.

He'd considered it wiping the slate clean.

And he couldn't tell if he was pleased to see Isabel now, or if it only added to how hollow he felt. How dark and empty, all the way through.

Constantine held himself tightly, as if standing at attention would make this confrontation easier. A confrontation he knew, if left to his own devices, he would have avoided forever.

"If you came here to thank me for not ruining you, or indeed to take me to task for coming so close in the first place, I'll save you the trouble." He inclined his head. It was not Molly's majestic act of kneeling, but then, he doubted he possessed her strength. "It is I who owe you an apology, Isabel. For too many things to count." The words he needed to say clogged his throat. They actually *hurt*, but he made himself say them anyway. "I am sorry, Isabel."

It occurred to him that it was possible she'd come here to gloat. To taunt him. To take a piece out of him for what he'd tried to do to her daughter as well as to her. And he would take it, because he'd earned it, and he—

"Oh, Constantine." Isabel let out a laugh that reminded him entirely too much of her daughter. It was warm and husky, filled with life even as it sounded a bit rueful. "You have always been so touchy, haven't you?"

If he stood any straighter he would break in half. "…touchy?"

The older woman sighed. She gestured toward the bed. "I come to see your mother all the time."

Constantine stared at her, because her words didn't make sense. On any level. Isabel Payne came to visit his mother? Whatever for? Dimly, the nurse's chatter about a Good Samaritan came back to him. Could it be?

He shook his head, baffled.

And found himself wholly unable to speak.

"She and I have a lot in common, for our sins," Isabel said, sounding far too wise for Constantine's taste. "I like to think we could have been friends, if things had been different."

"I'm not entirely certain my mother was capable of having friends," Constantine forced himself to say, as a kind of olive branch, though tearing the words out of him felt more like ripping trees apart than extending branches.

"Everyone is capable of having friends," Isabel replied. Her eyes were too blue. Too much like Molly's. Too capable of seeing straight through him. "But like most things, not just anyone will do. It has to be the right friends."

Isabel moved further into the room, holding herself like a person who had every expectation of being welcome wherever she went. Something, he could see now, she had handed down to her daughter, along with those blue, blue eyes. Because Constantine was the one who suddenly felt out of place. Who stepped back as if this was a hospital room Isabel belonged in, not him.

Which was currently also how his life felt around him. Misshapen, because Molly had been in the middle of it.

But then every muscle in him tensed up when Isabel reached out and laid her hand on his arm.

Her gaze on his was far too warm. Far too knowing.

"You should hate me," he gritted out. "Why don't you?"

"I have spent too much time being hated myself," she replied. "I would never inflict it on another. Or myself. What a waste. Might as well chain yourself to whatever you're hating and leap into the sea. That's the kind of power you give it."

Constantine thought of the stories Molly had told him about her childhood, more when she'd been sixteen than now. Back then he'd been far more interested in piecing those stories together to make them scandalous. *SAD SINGLE MUM TO SKALAS BRIDE! PREGNANT AT SIXTEEN!*

Only now did it occur to him that Molly had not been as naive as he'd imagined her back then. She had already faced all manner of close-minded ignorance. All he'd done was show her that such mean-spiritedness wasn't the unique province of small country villages.

He kept thinking it was impossible to hate himself more. And in that, too, he was wrong.

Isabel squeezed his arm and he stared down at her hand, still astounded that she had simply… reached out and touched him. As if he was a regular man instead of this monster he'd become.

A monster far too like his father.

"And I want to apologize to you, Constantine," she said softly. "I should have tried harder to get through to you, but not in my usual clumsy way. I know I only made things worse."

Constantine couldn't breathe. He couldn't cope with this. It was as if this woman was a tsunami, ripping into him years ago and now again, and in all this time he still hadn't figured out how to survive her.

Maybe he never would. Maybe all these years of plotting and planning and honing himself into what he'd thought was the perfect weapon for his revenge had all been leading here, to a quiet care facility and a soft hand on his arm.

Maybe he had always been meant to go out with a whimper, after all.

"Some people aren't worth these efforts, Isabel," he managed to say, though everything inside him seemed to rock wildly back and forth. "There's no getting through to them. No matter what you do, or what you try, it will always be futile. There's nothing clumsy or elegant that could ever be done to reach them where they've gone, and good riddance."

Isabel squeezed his arm again, as if that was a normal thing that people just…did. And worse, smiled at him. As if she couldn't see what a monster he was, when she should know better. When she'd been married to his father, the worst monster of all.

"I suppose vengeance can be elegant," she said as if this was nothing but happy cocktail chatter.

"It requires surgical precision, doesn't it? I think you'll find that in contrast, love is often clumsy, Constantine. Or it wouldn't hurt so much, would it?"

And it was not until that moment, with Isabel Payne's hand on his arm, his own mother there in the same room, and his heart flayed wide open, that Constantine understood at last.

He was in love.

All this time, all these years, all his grand plans…and he was *in love*.

And the moment that was clear to him, at long last, there was only one place for him to go.

CHAPTER ELEVEN

MOLLY WAS ENJOYING a quiet evening in—or more accurately, brooding with wine yet again, because that appeared to be all she did when left to her own devices since she'd returned from Paris—when a terrific pounding started up on her front door downstairs.

She had long since removed any buzzer from her property, because the paparazzi had regularly abused it. Anyone who wished to contact her should have her mobile number, and if they didn't, they shouldn't contact her. Packages and other such deliverables she had delivered to her agent's offices instead. Where they could be picked up at her leisure or delivered by messengers she recognized.

There was no reason anyone should be pounding on her door.

She set her wine aside and stalked across to the windows that opened up onto the balcony that sat up above the street. She stepped out, breathing in the warm air. It was full summer in England. Light held on until late and even though it was just as likely that it would take a cold turn by morning, it was impossible not to feel a bit giddy.

But when Molly peered over the side of her balcony to see who was abusing her front door, she found she did not feel giddy at all.

Because Constantine stood there. Staring up at her as if *she* had left *him*, naked in a bed in a different country.

"I thought my debt was paid in full," she said, her voice going a bit echoey against the cobblestones.

Or maybe she was feeling a bit wobbly herself. She was clinging to the rail, though she told herself it was because it was his neck she would like to wring, not because her knees felt much weaker than they ought to have.

Because Constantine was here. Here, at her door. And he looked even more darkly beautiful than she remembered.

And all she seemed to do was remember him.

She had spent a lot of time imagining him in different places, and different poses—and a thousand different *positions* because her body longed for him in ways that made her shiver—but she hadn't imagined him here. All of that simmering Greek glory, out on the cobblestones with London brooding about in the background. Rumpled and hot-eyed and almost too recklessly masculine to look at directly.

It was almost too much to take.

"This isn't about *debts*," he retorted.

A bit loudly, to her surprise.

Almost as if he…felt something.

But this was Constantine Skalas. There was more likely to be a sudden stampede of unicorns along her cobbled street than there was for him to catch a terrible case of *feelings*, like a bad flu. And it was even less likely that if he did, he would come here to share them with her.

After all, their relationship had been a lie when she was sixteen and more recently nothing but debts and dares. A *hetaira* indeed.

Because she'd looked that word up once she'd come home, thinking he'd used an endearment. She should have known better.

"Then there's no reason for you to be here, is there?" she asked coolly, glaring down at him. "After all, ours was a transactional relationship at best."

"I'm not here to talk about transactions!" he thundered at her.

Even more loudly.

She responded by going arctic. "My mistake. Are you here to *talk*? Do you do *talking*, Constantine? Is that part of your revenge fantasy?"

His eyes blazed. And she had the strangest notion he was about to explode. Right out in the open.

Molly wanted to see that more than she wanted her next breath. And equally wanted to protect him from it. She despaired of herself and her endlessly stupid heart.

"Do you truly wish to shout at each other?" he asked her, biting off each word as his gaze incinerated the world around him. "In public?"

And she had to think about it.

Because she was certain no good could come of letting that man into her house. No good could come of letting herself get close to him again. Physically, that was.

Does anyone get close to Constantine Skalas? the bitter voice inside her asked.

Still, the last thing she needed was to have someone make a video of this confrontation and splash it over the internet, which she knew they would. Because who needed the paparazzi when everyone had a mobile in their hand? She scanned the windows opposite her and didn't see any telltale twitching curtains, but that didn't mean anything.

Eyes were everywhere. That had been the first lesson Constantine had taught her.

She turned on her heel and slammed her way back into her house, running down the stairs to the front door and then waiting there a moment, desperately trying to get her breath under control.

But she gave it up as futile and tossed the door open.

Constantine brushed his way inside, then stood there, glowering at her in her own hallway as she slammed the front door shut, locking them in.

Together. And alone.

Not that it mattered if they were alone or with ten thousand people, surely. Not anymore.

Her heart, predictably, beat too hard anyway.

"There's no reason for you to be here," she told him, her voice hot and potentially unhinged, but she couldn't worry about that. "The note you left me in Paris did all the talking you could ever need to do. My debt was paid. Is that how a *hetaira*'s term was usually ended? I'm not conversant on the finer points of relinquishing a courtesan."

"A *hetaira* is not any old run-of-the-mill courtesan, Molly," he began, frowning at her.

"Did you really come here to debate the finer points of an ancient Greek insult you were using as an endearment?" She actually laughed, and not in a way that indicated she found anything funny. "Because I would rethink that approach, if I were you."

"You don't understand." He moved closer, but stopped, clearly reading the scowl on her face. Was she happy about that or disappointed? "Molly, you must know I didn't leave you because you were some kind of courtesan and I was finished. I left you for your own good."

It had to be said that she had not seen that one coming.

But she didn't like it any better for being unexpected.

"How noble." Her voice was scathing. "Next time, leave a tip."

His face darkened, and she hated the part of her that couldn't simply hate him the way she should. That wanted to make him feel better, even now.

"Everything I told you that night was the truth," he said, his voice as intense as it was rough. "And it is mine to regret that it took me so long to understand that in all this time, what I thought was vengeance was never that at all. Never. It would have been far easier for me if it was. My curse all along was that I never hated you or your mother the way I thought I should have."

That mapped a little too closely to what she'd been thinking, and she didn't trust the way her heart kicked at the idea of a connection between them.

She scowled to cover it. "You have a very funny way of showing it, then. And yes, I'm aware you made some restitution, but that's just money, Constantine. God knows you have far too much of that."

It occurred to her then, as he glared down

at her with too much of that ferocious intensity that shouldn't have stirred her at all, that she was trapped with her back to her own front door. She couldn't have that.

Molly pushed her way past him and didn't look back as she marched back up her stairs. Then into her great room, where she swept up her wine along with the bottle. And then stood there, glaring balefully, as Constantine followed.

Because it just wasn't fair. He had neglected to shave today and his jaw looked deliciously rough. His hair was its usual mess. He was wearing nothing interesting at all, a T-shirt and jeans, except it was instantly clear that neither item was the sort of thing a regular person could buy in a store. Just like he was no regular person.

He still looked like a statue that begged to be cast in marble. And now, despite everything, all she could think about was that she knew how he tasted. Every part of him. Looking at him again now, all she could think about was how he had moved inside her, changing everything.

Changing *her*.

And then he'd left her all the same. The way he'd warned her he would at the start.

He'd even warned her that she would fall for him.

And fool that she was, she had.

"I thought that you did it all rather beautifully,

really," she said as he stood there in the middle of the quiet, soothing retreat that she would now always remember with him in it. Damn him. She would have to move. "It all went according to plan. I knew better than to let my feelings get involved, and yet they did. And you left me, as you promised you would. Did you come here to pick apart the corpse?"

"Molly." Constantine's voice was urgent. His bitter coffee eyes wild. "I love you."

Something inside her detonated. She could feel it. But Molly didn't move, even as she felt everything inside her…liquefy. She clutched her wineglass in one hand, the bottle in the other, and thought very seriously about throwing the bottle directly at his head.

But she didn't.

She didn't know how she didn't.

"That's very flattering," she said, making her voice absolutely frigid. "But you don't."

"I do," he said, frowning at her with a certain level of arrogant outrage, no doubt because she hadn't flung herself prostrate on the floor before him in abject gratitude. "You must know that you're the only reason I have feelings in the first place. It took me a long time to realize what they were, that's all." He raked a hand through his hair. "I had to let go of my mother. I had to see her for who she was, not who I wished her to be.

I had to take a good, hard look at why I wanted her on a pedestal in the first place. But I did that, Molly. I did it and I even accepted how I felt about your mother, and why. When I tell you that I love you—"

Deep inside, she could feel a kind of tremor, but she fought it back.

And she had to shut him up before that tremor took her down. "Constantine. You're just talking about yourself. You can hear that, can't you? That's not love, I think you'll find. Though it might be some abnormal psychology that you should probably look into when you leave. Which I can only hope will be shortly."

He stared at her as if she was the one acting erratically.

"You are mistaken," he bit out. "I love you, Molly. I wonder if I always have."

He *wondered*.

Molly felt everything inside of her…blow up.

She thought of that girl, lost and lonely, torn away from everything she'd ever known and shunted off to that blinding island, with the Greek sun that blazed on her only one of the things that shined too brightly to look at directly. She thought of the horror she felt when she'd realized what Constantine was truly about, when she'd read those stories he'd placed. And all the contortions she had gone through to convince herself that it had all been her fault, not his.

Then there were all the years in between, where she had made herself into the very thing that girl could never have imagined she'd become. Anti-beige. Anti-porridge. And all along knowing, somewhere deep inside of her, that she was doing it because of him.

At him.

He had made her feel small, so she became giant.

Epic.

She remembered when it had begun to occur to her how strange it was that her mother kept having so many runs of notably bad luck when, whatever else Isabel was, she had never been stupid. And how Molly had felt when she'd traced it all back to Constantine himself.

When he'd made certain she could trace it back to him.

And she could remember with perfect clarity leaving this very house that morning, so long ago now, to fly down to Skiathos and face him at last.

Molly had known the truth then, hadn't she? She called it nerves. Anxiety. A history she wanted nothing to do with, she'd assured herself, but she'd known better.

She'd been excited.

Thrilled that she would see him again, at last, no matter the circumstances.

That was the long and the short of it. She had gone to Skiathos to confront him about the things he'd done to her mother and her, the campaign he'd deliberately waged against her family *for years*, and she'd been *excited*.

There had been those ten days spent naked in the sunlight, then dressed for his pleasure when the stars came out.

There had been their press tour, all those hours spent together flying from place to place, and the performance they both put on so well for the cameras. The *dancing*. The *gazing*.

All to be left on the very night she'd given him her innocence, called her a whore, and had abandoned her. Not in that order.

"The fact of the matter," she hurled at him, slamming the wine bottle down on the nearest table and slightly surprised it didn't shatter with the force she expended, "is that you should thank your mother. Because you've been using her as an excuse for your entire life."

"Molly—"

But she was just getting started.

"You focus with all your might on blame and retribution, because that's much better than asking yourself why it is you've been hiding behind that poor woman since you were a kid. Isn't it,

Constantine? You built a whole alternate persona based on sex and promiscuity, perceived indolence and carelessness. All the while hiding the truth of you, deep inside."

"That feels a bit pot and kettle, wouldn't you say?" he bit out. *"Magda?"*

"Magda is a stage name," she snapped out. "It's the difference between putting on a costume and taking one off, that's all. I'm not hiding anything, Constantine. I'm not two people. I'm not hiding in Magda—she's a part of me." And she knew as she said it that it was true. Maybe it hadn't always been true, but it was now. She leaned in. "She's always been a part of me. It's what I call the part of myself that can handle the bright lights, the applause, the strange and glorious things that come when your face is your currency. But that's not what you're doing."

"Oh no? Then what is it I'm doing, if you are suddenly the expert on healthy and unhealthy divisions of personalities."

"You'll do anything to avoid feeling an emotion," she said. Like she was handing down judgment. "Anything and everything. Everybody knows men who sleep around like that don't *feel*, so no one expects you might, do they? Boys will be boys and so on." She shook her head. "And left to your own devices, you think… You really, truly believe that a lifetime spent in a sick pursuit of vengeance against a stepmother who never did anything to you except try to take care of you is *love*."

He looked like he might explode. Or as if he had. As if this was the explosion. Maybe it had claimed them both already.

Molly realized she might not be able to tell.

"I just told you I loved you," Constantine thundered at her. "Do you think that's easy to say? Do you imagine that I've ever said it to another living human being? Because I haven't. It's only you, Molly. Don't you understand that yet? Whatever you call it, however twisted it's been, it's only ever been you. I love you, whether you believe that or not."

She didn't know where her wineglass had gone. Molly surged toward him, stopping herself just before she made a critical error and threw herself at him.

Because she knew, somehow, that would not end the way she wanted it to. She would not pummel him the way she wanted. She would end up kissing him and if she did, she would lose this moment forever.

Molly knew she couldn't allow that to happen.

"You need to feel all the parts of love, Constantine," she threw at him. "And you don't. You can't. It's not just sex. It's not just connection to another person. As wonderful as those things are, they're only one half of the whole. You have to feel its opposite." When he gazed back at her without comprehension, she made a small sound of frustration. "You have to feel the bad as well as the good to get the whole. Like loss."

He jolted as if she'd slapped him, with a wall or two in her hand. "I have no idea what you're talking about."

She moved closer to him, and she knew somehow, deep inside, that it was because she didn't know how to stay away.

But that was future Molly's problem.

"You loved your mother and you lost her," she said, very intently. "And I'm not pretending that's an easy thing. Or that I would know what to do if I lost my mother, because I know I wouldn't."

"My mother..." He shook his head. "I visited her just today. She—"

"You lost her," Molly said again. Firmly. "As far as I can tell, you lost her again and again. And so you blamed my mother. Then you blamed me. And you arranged your entire life around revenge—on me, because I made you feel something when you thought only she could."

"Not something," he gritted out at her. "*Love*, Molly."

"Have you ever stopped to take that in, Constantine?" she asked him then. "Have you ever allowed yourself a moment, just a single moment, to grieve?"

And she watched as that rocked over him. As he stood there before her, Constantine Skalas, rendered...not a devil. Not a scourge. Not the playboy or the reckoning.

He was no more and no less than a man.

At last.

My man, a voice in her said, with a kind of certainty that seemed to ring deep inside her, like a bell.

And she stayed where she was, holding her breath, as he visibly fought to accept what she'd said to him. While between them, all the fury and explosiveness seemed to ease, until it almost felt as if they were back in Greece. Where there was nothing but a breeze from the sea, faintly calling wind chimes, and the sunlight all over the both of them like a blessing.

He stood there like that for some time. And when he found her gaze again, she could have sworn there was a different man there behind those dark, rich eyes.

He reached over and ran a finger down one cheek, and her foolish heart lurched.

"Do you love me, Molly?" he asked her, his voice a rough scrape. "*Can* you love me?"

She might have fought on, had he thundered at

her some more. Had there been more of that exploding, that heat.

Had he not touched her like that, as if checking to see if she was real.

Had he not…simply asked.

"I should hate you," she whispered. "I want to hate you."

He nodded at that, a sharp movement. As if he had already accepted how this was going to go. Not in his favor.

"You have every reason to hate me. I can't blame you." He blew out a breath. "In fact, I think I ought to encourage you to hate me as much as possible. It's only what I deserve."

Molly searched his face, his dark gaze. Did she want to be strong—or did she want to be happy?

She knew the answer even as she asked it.

Carefully, deliberately, she reached across that space between them to take one of his hard, magical hands in hers.

"I've been really, really bad at hating you, Constantine. For as long as I've known you. I'm afraid it just doesn't stick." She looked down at his hand, because there was too much emotion behind her eyes and thick in her throat. "If you want the truth, I've been in love with you since I was sixteen years old. And all these things you've done to me, I forgave a long time ago. I suppose that makes me as naive and stupid as I've ever been, but that doesn't make it any less true. Even if it is naivete, well, I prefer it to the sad and jaded alternative."

It seemed to her like an eternity, though likely no more than a second before his fingers were on her chin, tipping it up so that he could look at her directly. So he could look *into* her, she thought, as her breath caught.

"I love you, Molly," he said, as if he was taking a solemn vow. "I've never loved anyone else. I've never known how. And I'm nothing if not single-minded. If you let me, I will dedicate my life to learning how to love you so well, so deeply, and so perfectly, that you never question for a moment that you are anything but adored. Never stupid. Never naive. Simply mine, from the start."

She blew out a breath, feeling that tremor inside of her loom again, but Molly knew what it was now. She wasn't afraid of it.

There was heat, and her endless need for him. And beyond that, or mixed in with it, that *something else* that had always been there. That had pushed her along this path until she'd found him again. That had made her *excited* to face him in Skiathos when she should have been anything but.

And she'd named it now, hadn't she? Or he had.

It was love. It had always been love.

Just waiting there all this time for the two of them to see it.

"You silly man," she said softly, and smiled

when his arrogant brow rose. Because he was still Constantine Skalas, after all. And would she love him if he wasn't? "You're here. You came after me and thundered in the street. You look tortured, as you should. And I'm tempted to say I already feel sufficiently adored."

"That's just the beginning, Molly," he promised her hoarsely.

"But," she interrupted him. She pulled her chin out of his grasp and smiled at him in the cool way she knew he would take as a challenge. And sure enough, saw his gaze grow brighter. "I'm afraid there are consequences for outrageous revenge plots."

"Consequences?" he repeated.

"In life, there are always consequences, Constantine," she said breezily, echoing something he'd said to her what seemed like a lifetime ago. "You might not like them, but there are consequences all the same."

He considered her for a long moment, and then, slowly and wonderfully, he grinned.

"Never let it be said that Constantine Skalas cannot face the necessary consequences of his choices," he drawled. "I live for them, in fact."

"I'm glad to hear it." She gave him her most imperious, most Magda look. "Why don't we start with a little abject groveling?"

"I wouldn't know where to begin," he said, though his eyes gleamed.

"I think you do know," she said. She waved a languid hand. "You can start naked, obviously. And we'll move along from there."

Constantine's grin widened. She thought he might balk, but instead, he merely stripped off his T-shirt and tossed it at her. Molly found herself laughing as she batted it away from her face, and then she stood there, feeling buoyant and joyful and fizzy with it, as he toed off his shoes, rid himself of his jeans, and then presented himself before her, beautifully naked.

And undeniably hers.

"This is a very good start indeed," she told him.

"You have no idea."

And then Constantine showed her his version of a grovel.

He knelt there before her, drawing one leg over his shoulder so he could lick her straight over the edge.

Into her first hint of forever.

And true to his word, that was only the beginning.

CHAPTER TWELVE

TEN YEARS LATER, Constantine sat on the lowest terrace down the cliff from his Skiathos house, waiting for his wife.

These days, he savored the waiting period.

First Molly had taught him to love. Then she taught him to grieve, and he had. It had taken time. It had been a journey, as he'd learned grief often was. Nor did it ever go away. Not really.

But only once he'd allowed himself to truly face what he had lost had he found hope. Laughter. And the wholeness of love. The good and the bad all mixed in together to make a life.

There, in the arms of this woman he did not deserve, who had forgiven him and loved him and given herself to him like pearls before the swine he was, Constantine Skalas learned at last how to be himself.

Just him.

For her.

The path had not always been easy. But then, what worth having in this life was ever easy?

They'd fought. They had gone through dark times both of their making and imposed upon them from without, but they'd come through it stronger. Closer.

All of it possible because of Molly, Constantine knew.

He became a brother to Balthazar, and in time, a friend. He and Molly had married on the same island where Balthazar had taken his own bride, and all four of them found a new future. And built a new kind of Skalas family, drenched deep in the love they'd worked so hard to find.

When their mother finally slipped away, some five years ago, Balthazar and Constantine had stood together, shoulder to shoulder, and allowed themselves to mourn.

Constantine and Molly had spent this far brighter decade building themselves the marriage they wanted. Then adding to it with the children Constantine had only ever wanted with her. Molly had retired Magda when she felt the time was best, and was considering the many offers she'd received, looking for what moved her. In the meantime, she was as stunning as he'd imagined she'd be, big with his daughters. Three in rapid succession, and then a squalling little thunderstorm of a son to cap off their collection.

And with Isabel as their magical, marvelous grandmother, Constantine knew that his son and his daughters would live the kind of life he could admit, now, he wished he'd had all along. His children were loved, and they knew it. His children were happy, and he worked hard to make sure they would always remain as close to that state as possible.

His children saw, every day, that he loved and honored and respected their mother. And that she loved him back. That their parents laughed and danced, fought and made up, and always, always, put each other and the family first.

He couldn't wait to see who they became, these four bright souls he would let nothing crush.

But Skiathos was for him and Molly alone.

He heard her on the path, as he always did. And when he turned to enjoy her approach by the light of all those same gently glowing lanterns, he smiled.

For she had worn the filmy, see-through gown he'd left out on their bed, so he could see her beautiful figure. Her curves were rounder now, after the four children she'd borne him, and her smile was brighter. Because here, and always, she was his.

And he was hers, entirely.

Love kept getting better all the time.

"You almost kept me waiting, *hetaira*," he murmured as she came to him, here in the place where they came to lie naked beneath the sun and remind themselves of all the ways they'd untwisted each other over the years.

"Never fear," she said as she approached. "I will always be your courtesan, my love. Especially here. Ready and willing to accept whatever consequences you render for the unpardonable sin of *almost* making you wait, the horror."

"And I will always be your husband, Molly," he replied, a vow he could never make enough. "A role I hope I will one day deserve."

She settled herself in his lap and gazed down at him with those arctic blue eyes that warmed for him. Always for him. He saw their past, their future. This beautiful present in these days they liked to steal for themselves, just the two of them, so they would always remember.

Not that he would ever forget.

And then the love of his life, the mother of his children, his perfect *hetaira*, kissed him as if she was breaking a spell. Or casting a new one.

The way she did every day.

And Constantine kissed her back with a hunger that only grew, year by year.

While all around them the lanterns glowed, the sea whispered far below, and forever was right here, tangled up between them and stretching out into eternity.

No revenge necessary.

Only love.

* * * * *

Couldn't get enough of
Her Deal with the Greek Devil?
*Look out for the first instalment in
the Rich, Ruthless & Greek miniseries,*
The Secret That Can't Be Hidden.

*And why not dive into these other stories
by Caitlin Crews?*

Claimed in the Italian's Castle
Christmas in the King's Bed
His Scandalous Christmas Princess
Chosen for His Desert Throne

All available now!

#3917 FROM EXPOSÉ TO EXPECTING
by Andie Brock

Following one sexy night with Leonardo, journalist Emma is left mortified by his swift rejection. Letting off steam, she writes a private, scandalous exposé on the tycoon...that's accidentally *published*! Yet that's nothing compared to the surprise that follows...

#3918 THE PLAYBOY'S "I DO" DEAL
Signed, Sealed...Seduced
by Tara Pammi

Dev Kohli's superyacht is the perfect hideout from the forced marriage Clare Roberts is escaping—despite the intimacy it brings... But when the threat to her increases, so does the need to protect her with something Dev never thought he'd offer—his ring!

#3919 HIS BILLION-DOLLAR TAKEOVER TEMPTATION
The Infamous Cabrera Brothers
by Emmy Grayson

Everleigh Bradford's lost too much already to simply hand over control of the family vineyard she expected to inherit. If she must confront internationally renowned new owner Adrian Cabrera, she will! *And* fight her red-hot response to the brooding Spaniard...

#3920 QUEEN BY ROYAL APPOINTMENT
Princesses by Royal Decree
by Lucy Monroe

As a naive teenager, Lady Nataliya signed a contract promising her to a prince. Now to release them both, she causes a scandal. It works... Until her betrothed's brother, the irresistibly brooding King Nikolai, insists she honor the marriage agreement—with *him*!

"Mr. Cabrera?"

The husky feminine voice slid over his senses and sent a flash of
heat over his skin. He took another deliberate sip of his wine before
turning his attention to the second woman who had invaded his
space this evening.

Her.

His eyes drifted back up to her face in a slow, deliberate perusal.
Lush silver-blond curls enhanced her delicate features. Violet eyes
stared back at him, and her caramel-colored lips were set in a firm
line.

"Yes," he finally responded, his voice cool, showing that, despite
the unusually intense effect she was having on him, he was still in
control.

She stepped forward and held out her hand, bare except for
a simple silver band on her wrist. Adrian grasped her fingers,
pleasantly surprised by her firm grip.

"My name is Everleigh Bradford. Congratulations on your
merlot. It's exquisite."

"Thank you." He arched a brow. "While your compliments are
appreciated, was it necessary for you to ignore the balcony-closed
sign and invade my privacy?"

Everleigh's chin came up and her eyes flashed with stubborn fire.
"Yes."

Intriguing… There were plenty of men who would have cringed at the slightest hint of his disapproval. But not this woman. She stood her ground, shoulders thrown back, lips now set in a determined line.

"You're a busy man, Mr. Cabrera. I need to speak with you on an urgent matter. I'm sorry for breaking the rules, but it was necessary for me to have a moment alone with you."

Her honesty was refreshing. A night with someone as bold and beautiful as Everleigh would more than make up for his past few months of celibacy.

He infused his smile with sensuality as he raked his gaze up and down her slim form once more, this time letting his appreciation for her body show. "I would greatly enjoy a moment alone with you."

Everleigh's cheeks flushed pink. The blush caught Adrian unawares. Was she an innocent or just playing a role? Much as it would disappoint him, she wouldn't be the first to go to such lengths to catch his attention.

"This has nothing to do with sex, Mr. Cabrera."

"Adrian."

Her lips parted. "I… Excuse me?"

"Please call me Adrian."

Those beautifully shaded violet eyes narrowed. "This is a business discussion, Mr. Cabrera. First names are for friends and family."

"We could become friends, Everleigh."

What was wrong with him? He never teased a woman like this. He complimented, touched, seduced… But with this woman he just couldn't help himself.

Perhaps it was the blush. Yes, that had to be it. The delicate coloring that even now crept down her throat toward the rising slopes of her breasts…

"We will never be friends, Mr. Cabrera," Everleigh snapped. "I'm here to discuss your proposed purchase of Fox Vineyards."

"Then let's talk."

Don't miss
His Billion-Dollar Takeover Temptation.
Available June 2021 wherever
Harlequin Presents books and ebooks are sold.

Harlequin.com

HPEXP0521